For the Love Of a Woman

S. Anne Gardner

ISBN 0-9744121-6-3
First Printing 2004
Cover art and design by Anne M. Clarkson
Photos by Catherine De Souza

Published by:
Dare 2 Dream Publishing
A Division of Limitless Corporation
Lexington, South Carolina 29073
Find us on the World Wide Web
http://www.limitlessd2d.net

Printed in the United States of America and the UK by

Lightning Source, Inc.

IV

Acknowledgements

To my four little loves,

To J, whose love never wavers and whose arrival was a gift in my life. You my darling kept me human through all the cold and lonely years and taught me how much love I was capable of towards one human being. Your hand has always been in mine as my love will always be yours.

To C, all my memories of you are filled with such love and beauty. One day when we are but golden clouds upon the wind, I shall be with you again. My heart still aches for you my dearest darling boy. A part of me went to heaven with you. I gave you the music to take with you till we are once more together again.

To L, you taught me that miracles are possible with your arrival. You fill my life with such wonder and hope. You touch my heart in so many ways my darling. My life is so full because of you. I am always surprised with the beauty of your soul.

To A, you are such a blessing in my life. You touch my heart in so many ways. I look at you and I am filled with such joy. Your arrival gave me the strength and the belief that miracles come in more than ones. You are such a wonder my little darling. You my little man completed my life.

And to my little loves to come....you are the new twinkles in my eyes.

VI

Thank You's

Thank you to Lisa for the editing and the patience of having to deal with my tumultuous impassioned objections to making truly a great final product. You deserve this recognition more than you know.

Thank you to you Anne for the cover. It is truly exquisite. Your talent is only surpassed by your graciousness.

My thanks to Char, who believed in this story enough to propose its publication. Thank you for the belief and for the support of this project.

To Hope my thanks for listening to the endless rewrites and thank you for the steadfast friendship.

Thank you to Alina, my dearest and oldest friend who has always been their in the best and worst times in my life. You have always been a constant.

Thank you to my mother, who does not understand but loves me anyway. I learned how to be strong from her. She taught me to see the good and leave the bad behind.... Sorry it took me so long to finally understand you. I love you Mom.

And my very special thanks to all the Gems at the Gemini page.... Thank you for the belief, the e-mails.... Thank you for all the encouragement and the endless positive comments.... You are all truly special.

And thank you to all the fans that have taken the time to write me and to encourage me to keep on writing.

<u>Dedication</u>

To Lisa... my friend, my love, my lover and my wife who makes all my dreams possible. The day I married you I touched the heavens.

This book is dedicated to you, my dearest darling.... You inspired it...you who brought all my passion and my belief in a tomorrow filled with love and dreams to a reality. Because of you, this book was written. Because of you, I dream and write still. I no longer travel alone in this world and I am finally complete. Your hand is always in mine and my heart is safely kept and treasured in your body since it is one with yours. Thank you for all the years, for all the patience, for all the faith and all the laughter. And thank you for coming into my life. Thank you my dearest darling for looking beyond the image and seeing me.

I live, love, dream, hope and soar ever higher in a world with you and for you.

Yours forever and always,

S.

Chapter One

Raisa Andieta was the most infuriating, egotistical, arrogant, rude woman she had ever had the misfortune to meet. From the first moment they had met, it had been instant combustion. She had never reacted to another human being as she did with Raisa. The woman just knew how to push all of her buttons. And now they were on opposing sides again.

The first time Carolyn had met Raisa had been two years earlier when she and her family had arrived in Venezuela. The oil company that Matt, her husband, worked for had hosted a party for all their new executives. Raisa Andieta was the president and a major stockholder of Copeco Oil. Carolyn remembered the moment as if it had been yesterday. Matt had been introducing her to some of his colleagues when she turned around and met the bluest eyes she had ever seen. For one brief moment, she had felt suspended in time. The only way to describe the woman in front of her was breathtakingly beautiful.

Matt introduced her to Raisa. When they shook hands, Carolyn felt a jolt that made her whole body come alive. The reaction had been mutual; Carolyn had seen it in Raisa's eyes. After that brief moment of the strangest connection, the women had been like vinegar and oil. Whenever one was in the room, the other one knew and reacted to it. At first, Carolyn tried to talk to the aloof Ms. Andieta. But after a few ungracious and downright rude

1

reactions from Raisa, Carolyn just stopped trying. They had both drawn an invisible, antagonistic line.

Carolyn was somehow not surprised when Ester Curbelo, the wife of one of Matt's associates, told her that Raisa had come to the County Club and would be attending their meeting to voice her disapproval of the proposal on the agenda being voted on that night. Carolyn was furious. She had been working on this proposal for over three months, and she was sure that Raisa had known it was to be voted on that night. There was nothing that Raisa did not seem to know. She reigned in this part of the country with an iron hand. If she wanted something done, it got done. If she wanted something to cease, it would, probably within minutes of the voicing her desire.

The project that Carolyn had been working on would bring much needed resources to the poor of the city of Caracas. It was a different way of distributing and allocating resources, but she believed it would be more efficient and that those who really needed it would receive aid even more quickly. The way things had been done for the last 10 years had not been as efficient as the new plan. The population had changed, the needs had changed and the money was being mismanaged. If Raisa Andieta had been at all approachable Carolyn felt sure she would have convinced her of this. She had actually tried to set up an appointment to discuss it with her and Raisa Andieta had agreed to meet with her. Carolyn still remembered the humiliating way that she had been treated.

Carolyn had arrived ten minutes early to the appointment with Raisa to discuss the Club's project. She waited for fifty minutes before she was ushered to the mighty Ms. Andieta.

Carolyn stood in front of her desk and Raisa continued to look at the papers in front of her, ignoring the other woman's presence completely. After a few minutes Carolyn's temper got the better of her and she simply sat down and played the silent game as well.

Raisa then sat back in her chair, crossed her legs, and looked at Carolyn with a very pleased smile on her face.

"Please, do sit down," said Raisa sarcastically.

"Thank you, I think I will," Carolyn answered with a smile.

Raisa stood up and walked around the room silently, just

staring at Carolyn.   She finally stood behind Carolyn and asked seductively "What do you want?"

Carolyn said nothing for a moment. She could feel Raisa looming above her.   She could swear that she heard the beating of Raisa's heart or was it her own?   For a moment they both shared the silence.   The air suddenly became very charged and a feeling of giddiness started to fill her being. She could feel the heat of Raisa's body behind her, and her senses filled with her fragrance.

Carolyn took in a large breath and stood quickly, facing Raisa. She felt disoriented and confused.   All of a sudden the room began to spin and she reached for the back of the chair in front of her.

Raisa reacted quickly and closed the distance between them. She held Carolyn closely to her. At that moment the room seemed to close in on them and all Carolyn felt was the warmth of Raisa's arms as her head fell back and her knees gave way.

"Sit down," Raisa said softly, guiding Carolyn back to the chair. She gently brushed Carolyn's hair away from her face; her touch was softness itself. All that Carolyn saw were those blue eyes, those eyes that were now hovering over her face. Her tongue came out and wet her lips as her ears filled with the loud pounding of her heart as Raisa's face came even closer.

Carolyn's eyes closed, as she whispered an anguished "No." When she opened them again she saw Raisa walking over to the bar on one side of her office and brought back a glass of water.

"Drink this, Cara," she whispered as she sat down in the chair next to Carolyn.

Carolyn held the glass with a shaky hand. Raisa, noticing the nervousness, then placed her hand over Carolyn's and guided the glass to her mouth. "Try to drink most of it."

Carolyn drank most of the water and as she finished her eyes sought those of the woman next to her.

For a moment they both looked at each other in silence.

"I'm so sorry, I don't know what happened to me," Carolyn said quickly. Her eyes looked down to the two hands still holding the glass. She looked away but not before Raisa saw the fear and the confusion in her eyes.

Raisa curtly released her hand and stood up. As she walked away she said, "Don't you?" loud enough for Carolyn to hear, and then went to sit behind her large desk.

Raisa now stared at her as she sat behind the authority of her large desk and the distance between them was once again palatable.

Carolyn looked up in confusion. Raisa's eyes became glacial.

"What do you want?" She asked impatiently.

The aggressiveness of the statement took Carolyn by surprise. Just a moment ago this same woman had been tender and caring. Her surprise must have shown in her semblance because Raisa reacted to it right away.

"I don't have all day, Mrs. Stenbeck." Raisa became visibly agitated and fidgeted.

Carolyn just stared for a moment. "I wanted to discuss a project I have been working…" Before she was able to finish, she was cut off.

"Mrs. Stenbeck, what do you think I do here all day? Run along to one of your lunches and do not take up any more of my valuable time! I don't have time to listen to your little projects." Raisa glared at her, having effectively dismissed her.

Carolyn was stunned. Her surprise was quickly replaced with rage. She stood up, shaking, not quite sure if she was still in a daze or just shaking from pure anger. She opened her mouth to say something but could not get past her outrage. She felt the glass in her hand and looked down at it.

She threw the remains of the water on Raisa who stood up in stunned shock.

"There! Maybe that will cool you off a bit!" On that note, Carolyn walked out of the office.

For days Carolyn expected Matt to come home and tell her he had been fired. She still could not believe what she had done. She had never reacted to another person the way she always seemed to react whenever she and Raisa were in the same room. Carolyn realized she had gone too far that day. She never told Matt what happened that afternoon and apparently neither did Raisa Andieta.

From that day on, Carolyn avoided all type of contact with Raisa. Whenever there was a dinner or an event that Raisa was to attend she was careful to come up with some excuse not to go. And now they were back in the same position, both on opposite sides and both in the same room.

Chapter Two

Carolyn knew that her proposal was pretty much dead. If Raisa Andieta objected to it that was far as it would go. No one would ever argue it. This was the power that Raisa wielded. Everyone knew it. No one fought her on anything. No one tried to; no one except Carolyn Stenbeck had ever tried to.

Most of the wives of Ms. Andieta's executives had learned to just bow and follow very quickly; all but Carolyn Stenbeck, that is. She had been the exception. Walking into the reserved conference room of the exclusive Country Club, Raisa was quickly surrounded by the social climbing wives of her executives. At least that is how Raisa viewed them. She was aloofly polite and, as usual, her eyes scanned the room as she spoke until she found what her eyes sought at every function and, of late, never found: Carolyn Stenbeck. Then she saw her, just as she exited the room to one of the outdoor balconies.

****

Caracas by night was a magical city of lights. And, like magic, it was all illusion. In the daytime you could see more clearly, as all those magical little lights became small little hobbles stacked one on top of the other.   It was a mountain of poverty, crime and hunger that knew no relief and had very little hope.

Carolyn leaned against the balcony of the Country Club, aware that in its confines of wealth she was not affected.   Here, behind the walls of power and excess, she was protected.   She felt a twinge of sadness.   She had worked so hard on this proposal.   This had been something of her own.   Something that would have helped all those people.   And now things would continue as they always had.   As much as Carolyn tried she had never quite fit into this society.   Matt was always busy.   Simon, her 8-year-old son was her pride and only joy.   Matt had stopped being the man she had loved a long time before.

Carolyn felt restless and unfocused.   This move to Caracas two years ago had been a last ditch attempt to save her marriage for Simon's sake.   It was a new start and the money that Matt was making meant that Simon could have the best of everything. Carolyn, however, had left behind her friends, her family and her career.   She had looked forward to doing something useful, something like helping those poor people.   And now she would once again fill her days with all those banal things she hated so much.

She took comfort in the warm breeze as she stood on the verandah.   She was facing the city and as the breeze caressed her body she looked up to the stars.   Carolyn Stenbeck was a vision of beauty.   Her pale skin had become bronzed during the time she had been living in Venezuela.   Her golden hair had become streaked with the kiss of sunlight.   And in her white dress she was very much as some goddess of old must have been while worshipping the moon.   She closed her eyes and just gave herself to the sensations, hoping that the night would soothe her disappointment.

That was the vision that Raisa Andieta was faced with as she too walked out onto the verandah.   Carolyn had her arms around her body as her face looked to the night sky.   Raisa just stood still, watching her, mesmerized yet again.   She had told herself so many times that this woman had no special power.   She argued with herself incessantly.   Carolyn Stenbeck was no different than any other woman.   And yet, every time she went into a room she searched for her and was disappointed when she realized that

6

Carolyn was not there.

Raisa feasted on what she saw. She felt an undeniable pull towards this woman who, although beautiful, infuriated her each and every time she came close to her. Raisa had learned to keep her distance and yet her body only knew that **it** must seek what she wanted to run from.

Carolyn felt her before her eyes saw her. They were both enveloped with the glow of the moon and the music that played from within.

Raisa slowly approached her and then, looking out into the city, she stood by Carolyn's side in silence.

"The thing about these types of nights is that they are deceptive," Raisa said softly. Carolyn then turned and looked out onto the city as well.

"What do you mean?"

"One moment it's all calm and then the heavens open up and we drown."

Carolyn turned her head to look at her. Raisa was in some ways an enigma to her. She was as unreadable to her as this land that she had been living in for the past two years.

"I don't understand."

"Don't you?" Raisa turned to face Carolyn.

"Why must you always answer a question with a question?" Carolyn said with troubled eyes. The nervousness in the pit of her stomach started, as it always did within minutes of her proximity to Raisa Andieta.

"Why do you always provoke me?"

"Me?"

"Yes! You!" Raisa raised her arms in a gesture of frustration.

"Me? Me! It is you! You are the one who takes joy in humiliating me!"

Raisa stared at her without saying a word. All she saw was Carolyn's mouth and she wanted to know how it tasted. Raisa did an about face and took a few steps away from Carolyn. She stopped for a moment and then suddenly turned to face her again. Her eyes were focused. Carolyn stood her ground.

"I don't like cowardice," Raisa said beneath her breath. Her eyes spoke of hunger and something else that Carolyn could not understand.

"I am no coward, Ms. Andieta." This time she would not budge. Raisa had been looking for a fight and she was going to get one.

"You ran from that meeting."

"And who would fight you?" Carolyn said sarcastically. "No one. Not one of those women would have supported me against you. They would let all those people go hungry rather than oppose you. How do you feel, Ms. Andieta? How does it feel to have all that power to say who lives and who dies?"

"You are being dramatic! If you believed in what you were proposing you would have tried."

"And fight you?" Carolyn turned her back to her and took a few steps away, then laughed harshly.

"You have tried before," Raisa said menacingly. "Obedience is something you haven't learned…. yet."

Carolyn turned around quickly. She had had enough. "Go to hell! I am no one's chattel!"

"One day someone is going to tame you," Raisa said softly.

"Well, it won't be you!"

As soon as those words left her mouth the sky was lit with a flash of lighting and the thunder that followed was deafening. But all Carolyn saw was the fire that went out of control in the eyes of the woman standing before her.

Without seeming to move, Raisa came closer, pulling Carolyn hard against her own body. The sky above them was exploding as Raisa's mouth found its target. They were encompassed in a wind that rose from the earth and the hunger of the storm could be tasted in their mouths.

Raisa was taking and devouring Carolyn's lips and squashing all protests in its wake. Her hands sought to touch and feel. Raisa felt a hunger unlike any she had ever experienced. She had always taken what she wanted and she had hungered for this woman too long.

Carolyn was breathless, overpowered by the heat growing and welling up inside her. She was fighting not only Raisa's desire but also her own shock.

"No!" Carolyn tried to break away from Raisa's hold.

"Coward!"

And again the lighting flashed, followed by the sounds of thunder, as nature kept pace with the storm raging within them.

Raisa pushed Carolyn to a corner of the verandah against a wall.

"Let me go!" Shouted Carolyn into the storm.

Raisa smiled, placed her hand on Carolyn's breast, and squeezed.

Carolyn's hand flew through the air in indignation and caught Raisa across the face. Raisa stared at her in shock and anger as she grabbed the hand with an iron grip.

Raisa's mouth once again covered Carolyn's and this time the kiss was brutal. It was not a kiss of passion but of domination and only total surrender would be acceptable.

Carolyn tasted the blood in her mouth and suddenly, quite tired, a sob escaped her lips.

Raisa pulled away immediately. She stared into Carolyn's eyes and saw them as they filled with tears of frustration. The storm was howling around them and yet, suddenly, all stood still between them.

"Let me go'" As in a vacuum, all seemed soundless. It was only the two of them. One body pressed against the other. One was holding the other prisoner.

Slowly, Raisa lowered her hands and watched as Carolyn ran away from her. Then suddenly, she turned and once again the world became the storm. She stood rooted to the spot, the wind blew around her, and the sky exploded over and over again. She faced the storm unafraid and challenged it. She was Raisa Andieta, and no one opposed her. She laughed out loud into the wind.

The storm had just begun.

S. Anne Gardner

Chapter Three

"Why are we having power problems, Joaquin?" Demanded Raisa of the executive standing nervously in her office.

"It's the rains, Ms. Andieta. Katya is having mudslides. There are no reliable reports as to the dead count. And all the power lines are taking the toll...."

"Joaquin, I don't care what is happening in Katya! We have a new generator, why are we having power problems!" Raisa yelled at the top of her lungs.

"It is being looked at, Ms. Andieta," he answered miserably.

"Go and make sure it gets done. Go!" She yelled, pointing to the door.

"Ms. Andieta..."

"Get out of here!" With that, the man almost ran out of her office.

Before having a moment to dwell in her anger, her phone buzzed. The phone in her office had been ringing incessantly all day.

"Yes, Gloria."

"Ms. Andieta, I have Matt Stenbeck on line two."

"All right, Gloria. Did he say what he wants?"

"Apparently they are having problems at one of the rigs."

"Damn! All right." Raisa switched lines. "Matt, what is going on?"

"Ms. Andieta, we had an explosion here at rig 31."

"You what?"

"The fire is under control now, but the rains have not helped."

"How did this happen, Matt? This is your rig, who is responsible for security there?"

"Alberto Curbelo handles security, but..."

"Fire him, security is compromised. I want him off the premises as soon as you hang up this phone and Matt, I want you here by tomorrow morning with the changes and upgrades."

"Ms, Andieta, we had casualties."

"Fire him. I want him off my rig. Do it, Matt."

She hung up the phone in aggravation. There were always casualties. That was just the way life was. In the end the profits outweighed the losses. In her opinion, the losses were an acceptable factor.

Her phone line buzzed again. "Yes, Gloria."

"Ms. Andieta, there has been a cave-in near Las Lomas. The street is underwater. They are reporting some drowning of people caught in cars." Gloria's voice was shaking

"Gloria, calm down. Get to the point!"

"The police called in to inform us that one of the cars caught in the cave-in was a company car." The secretary began to cry.

"Gloria! For the love of God! Stop your crying and tell me what else."

"Ester Curbelo and her two boys drowned. There was also another woman in the car with her that they have not identified yet."

"Keep me informed," Raisa said and then disconnected the call.

It had been raining for a week. There were mudslides all over the city. And now this. This would probably slow down the production timetables.

She remembered meeting Ester Curbelo. She had actually been pleasant enough to talk to, Raisa thought to herself. She was sorry about the boys and glad she had never met them.

Raisa remembered that she had always seen Ester at those

dinners she hated attending. And of course she remembered her because whenever Carolyn had attended she would be speaking to her. Carolyn!

There had been another woman in the car.

****

Raisa called Carolyn's house and the phone seemed to ring forever. Finally, someone picked up.

"Residencia Stenbeck, buenos dias."

"I want to speak to Mrs. Stenbeck."

"I'm sorry, Mrs. Stenbeck is not home."

"When will she be back? Do you know where she is?"

"She went out this morning and has not returned. I don't know when she will be home."

"Do you know if she spoke with Ester Curbelo today?"

"Who is this?" The maid asked suspiciously.

"Listen to me very carefully. I am Raisa Andieta. Do you recognize the name?"

"Yes, of course, Ms. Andieta."

"Then stop asking stupid questions and tell me if Carolyn spoke with Ester Curbelo today!"

There was a brief pause. "Yes, Ms. Andieta, she did."

"Dios Mio," escaped Raisa's lips. "If you hear from Mrs. Stenbeck tell her to contact me immediately, do you understand?"

"Yes, Ms. Andieta."

Raisa switched phone lines and dialed directly to the person she had inside the police department. She kept telling herself that she was overreacting. Just because Ester Curbelo had spoken with Carolyn this morning meant nothing. And yet she felt her heartbeat picking up and her breathing was becoming agitated.

The phone seemed to ring and ring. The longer it took before someone picked up the more agitated she became. Finally, someone picked up the receiver.

"Oigo, Sargento de Guardia."

"Ramiro, it's Raisa Andieta."

"Ms. Andieta, what a pleasure it is…"

"I want to know the names of all the people that were in my company car out at the cave-in at Las Lomas today."

"Ms. Andieta, please hold on and I will get that information."

"Fine, hurry."

Raisa waited tapping her fingernails on her desk. A few minutes later she was still waiting, becoming more anxious.

"Ms. Andieta?"

"Yes, I'm here."

"We have an Ester Curbelo and her two sons Paulo, 6 years old, and Andres, 4 years old. There is another woman and another child in the car that have not been identified as of yet."

"Ramiro, this is a priority. Find out who this other woman is. But most importantly I want you to find someone that is missing. Put all the men possible to this effort."

"Ms. Andieta, that may be difficult right now. Los barrios are collapsing with the water."

"No argument. I want this done, Ramiro. This is not a request. Do you understand?"

"Yes, Ms. Andieta. Who am I looking for?"

"Her name is Carolyn Stenbeck. Her son attends Campo Alegre School. Find her and call me immediately. Nothing is more important than finding this woman, do you understand?"

"Ms. Andieta…"

"Nothing or you are going to know what pain is."

"Yes, Ms. Andieta. I will put all my men on this."

Raisa hung up the phone and leaned back on her chair. Where was Carolyn?

****

Carolyn started getting really frightened as the water got higher and higher. There were cars both in front of her and behind her.

"I'm scared, Mommy," Simon whispered.

"Don't worry sweetheart. It's going to be okay. We will just be a little late in getting home." Carolyn tried to reassure him, but the more time that passed, the higher the water was getting. People started leaving their cars. She had to decide quickly.

"Mommy, the water is getting higher and higher, look! That car just fell into a hole!"

"Simon, put your window down, hurry!"

S. Anne Gardner

Chapter Four

Six hours later there still was no word of Carolyn. Raisa Andieta felt like she was about to jump out of her skin. She had never felt less in control. She had a million problems to deal with today, from generators to explosions, but she was used to working under incredible pressure. She had been grateful for the chaos; it had kept her focused. Every moment her mind was not over-filled she would come back to the knowledge that Carolyn was still missing and the woman in the car with Ester Curbelo had still not been identified.

Her phone buzzed and before the second ring she picked it up

"Yes, Gloria."

"Ms. Andieta, we have the numbers on the casualties at Katya."

"I don't give a fuck about Katya or all those people. Keep this line open for Ramiro Fonseca and him only. Do you understand?"

"Yes, Ms. Andieta."

"Have you kept calling Carolyn Stenbeck's home?"

"Yes, Ms. Andieta. Clara, the maid, says still no word from Mrs. Stenbeck."

"Keep calling the other numbers. She is the only other person I will answer calls from. Forward all else to Arturo Estes. Let him handle things for a change."

Yes, Ms. Andi--"

Before Gloria could finish the line went dead.

17

Raisa was pacing like a caged tiger. She faced the window and her emotions were as dark as the raging storm.

****

The phone rang on Raisa's private line and she pounced. "Hello."

"I have the information you requested."

"You know the name of the woman in the car?"

"Yes, Ms. Andieta."

Raisa took in a long deep breath and sat. She then held her breath. "What is it?" She said unable to recognize the tremor in her own voice.

"Her name was Maria Santisnero…" Raisa heard nothing else after that as her eyes closed in relief. "She was with her daughter Maite who was 6 years old. Apparently the two women always drove the children back and forth to school together."

"Ramiro, have you found me Carolyn Stenbeck?" Whispered Raisa weakly.

"We are still searching, Ms. Andieta. The city is in chaos. The list of people missing is growing as we speak. I have all my men looking for her. I wanted to give you an update."

"Ramiro, find her. Find her and I will give you 100,000 American dollars."

There was only shocked silence on the other side.

"Find her Ramiro. Find her for me."

"I will find her, Ms. Andieta." The line once again went dead.

Raisa sat behind her big desk and waited. Suddenly she realized that no one was calling for her. There was no one worrying whether she was home or not.

Most of the staff in the building stayed, not risking going out into the city, which was now in chaos. The building had been built to withstand all kinds of storms. If nothing else, Raisa Andieta liked efficiency. Everything had to work. The building had its own water system underground so it did not depend on the unreliable water system that serviced the city. It was also equipped with its own generators for emergency power.   Power outages were common but they did not effect the production of Copeco Oils Headquarters.   She had even gone as far as to set up separate phone systems to keep on top of news, not only out of the country but also within. Raisa knew power; she also knew how to wield it. And yet, with all this power at her disposal she could not find one single woman in a city.

A jeep had been kept waiting in case she had to move quickly. Another six hours and still no news. Raisa looked out into the storm again.

"Carolyn, where are you? What have you done to me? God, how I hate you!"

She walked over to the credenza and with one swipe of her arms all went flying.   The crashing of crystal brought a frightened Gloria into the private office.

"Ms. Andieta?"

Raisa leaned her forehead against the glass of the window. She closed her eyes and repeated softly.   "I hate you, Carolyn."

"Ms. Andieta?"

Raisa did not acknowledge her presence.   Gloria walked over to her boss cautiously. "Ms. Andieta?"

Raisa remained silent.   Gloria stood next to her now and touched her arm.

"Ms. Andieta? Are you all right?"

Raisa looked at Gloria as if for the first time.   She took a step away from the wall of glass.   She turned her back to Gloria and walked over the mess she had created, toward her desk, then sitting down behind her desk, she finally looked at Gloria.

"Get maintenance to clean this up." She began looking at some papers in front of her, ignoring the look of utter confusion on Gloria's face.

Gloria stood silently for a moment then rushed out to handle Raisa's request immediately.

****

An hour later Raisa's private phone rang again.

"Hello!"

"I found her, Ms. Andieta, she checked into the Caracas Hilton an hour ago."

"Thank God," she said as she sat down and covered her face with her hands.

Chapter Five

Carolyn could not believe she had made it this far. Luckily, she had had the foresight to grab her bag as she and Simon abandoned the car at the Autopista. There was water everywhere. Upon arriving she had heard that some people had actually drowned. She had managed to get a lift and then walk the rest of the way to the hotel. Simon was exhausted and frightened to death, the poor child. She had tried getting in touch with Matt but the hotel's phone lines were down.

Carolyn had walked into the Hilton carrying an exhausted child. They had been drenched to the bone and surely looked like two indigents. For a moment the desk clerk almost turned them away. Carolyn immediately showed her a credit card and booked a large suite and that, as always, took care of everything in Caracas.

First, she had taken care of Simon by bathing him and ordering room service. Then, she showered and now they were both wearing terry cloth robes from the hotel. Almost before he finished eating, Simon was sound asleep. She carried him into the second bedroom and shut the door as she walked out to the sitting room.

Carolyn finally allowed the toll the day had taken to come out. She no longer needed to be strong for Simon. When she and Simon jumped out of the car she had been faced with chaos everywhere. People were screaming because the street was collapsing and they were almost knocked down into the murky water as they ran. She had never been more terrified in all her life. Then, as they slowly made their way, darkness started to cover everything. Some parts of the city lost power and it became all the more frightening in the dark.

They had walked for hours until she had to carry Simon because he was too tired to walk anymore. They must have had a guardian angel because although they had somehow walked in the storm through the most dangerous parts of Caracas they had not met with any other problem other than that caused by the storm itself. As they got closer to the middle of town some streetlights were actually lit. By good fortune, she had seen a cab and it stopped. She offered the driver $500 to take her to the Caracas Hilton. It took them an hour to get there, but at last they were safe and indoors.

Carolyn sat down and raised her legs up. She curled up like a frightened child and allowed herself to cry. She was tired and exhausted and her emotions were raw. But mostly, she felt alone.

She became oblivious to everything around her until a constant buzzing broke her concentration. She looked at the door and realized someone was calling her name.

"Carolyn, Carolyn for God's sake, open the door!"

Carolyn got up and almost ran. She swung the door wide open. Neither woman knew who had moved first, but within a second Raisa was holding Carolyn tightly to her.

Carolyn's body started shaking as she began to sob.

"You're safe now, Cara. You're safe," Raisa whispered into her hair. "It's over. It's over." Carolyn raised her face and looked into Raisa's eyes.

Raisa's thumb caressed the tears away as her mouth lightly brushed Carolyn's lips. She pulled her again into her embrace. "You are exhausted. Come Cara, I will take care of you," Raisa said gently.

Carolyn was exhausted. She had reached the limits of her grip on things. Burying her face in Raisa's neck, she allowed the warmth of the arms that held her and the softness of the body against her to take over.

"Where is Simon?"

"He's asleep. Raisa, we almost drowned. It was horrible."

Carolyn began to weep again.

"I know Cara, I know. But you are safe now." Raisa turned and closed the door to the suite, which had remained open. "Which bedroom is he in?"

"That one," Carolyn answered with barely a whisper as she pointed to where Simon slept. "He was frightened to death. I hate living here. I want to go home. I hate living here."

Carolyn again allowed herself to be led in a protective embrace into the bedroom.

"We can talk about where you want to live tomorrow Cara, tomorrow. I want you to lie down Cara, what you need right now is rest." Raisa stood before Carolyn in the dark. As she stepped away Carolyn reached for her in fear.

"Don't go! Please, don't go!"

"I'm going to stay with you. I'm not leaving you." Raisa reassured her as her hand caressed Carolyn's face softly.

Raisa helped Carolyn to get under the covers. She then stepped away and started removing her own clothes. Carolyn waited quietly. Raisa got under the covers and as soon as she turned and opened her arms Carolyn was in them. Raisa stroked her hair slowly until she could hear that Carolyn's breathing had calmed down. Finally, she fell asleep.

Raisa held her as the storm continued beating outside. Never had she held a woman solely to comfort her. She had always taken pleasure. She had enjoyed both men and women, but she had to admit if given the choice she preferred women as lovers. Although, it was always harder to get rid of a woman lover after they had grown to be tiresome; more so than a man.

From the moment she met Carolyn Stenbeck, Raisa had wanted her. And normally she would have followed her hunger. But from the very beginning something inside told her to stay away. Then, of course, there was Carolyn herself. They seemed to disagree on everything. Carolyn wanted to change things, and Raisa hated anyone meddling and disrupting things she had been planning for. She could have transferred Matt Stenbeck many times over. And yet, she never had. Even after Carolyn had the gall to empty a glass of water by throwing it at her. She would have killed anyone else.

Raisa looked down at the woman who held onto her and something inside her began to grow and spread. Carolyn was clinging to her. She tightened her arms and put her face into Carolyn's hair as she dozed off to sleep with the thought that Carolyn Stenbeck was clinging to her and she had not pushed her away.

Chapter Six

A loud roar, followed by a flash of light that invaded the room, awakened Carolyn. She sat up in bed, fearful. She looked towards the curtains and could see the lightning flashes. It was still thundering. Suddenly she felt herself being pulled back into a warm embrace and she turned into it. She went into the safety of the warmth.

Carolyn's head was on the pillow as another flash of lightning made Raisa's face above her visible. "I'm here with you, Cara. I'm here with you." Carolyn heard Raisa's melodic voice speak to her, softly. She felt her robe being opened and pushed aside. Her skin seemed to be on fire. As she felt warm lips on her neck her mouth opened and welcomed that warm mouth with her own as Raisa's body laid on top of her.

****

"Mommy...Mommy," she heard from beyond the distance. Carolyn stirred and a feeling of well being spread a smile over her face as she went further into the warmth of the arms that embraced her.

"Mommy…"

Carolyn's eyes opened slowly as she heard the jiggling of the doorknob. "I'm coming, sweetheart," she responded half between sleep and wakefulness. She allowed herself one more intake of breath into the warmth of the embrace she was in.

"I think Simon is hungry," a soft voice said in her ear followed by a kiss.

Carolyn's eyes flew wide open and pulled away from the arms that held her. She stared at the face now fully in view in front of her in shock.

"Good morning," Raisa purred.

Carolyn was about to say something when the doorknob jiggled again. "Mommy?"

Carolyn became visibly nervous and once again stared at Raisa then back at the door.

"Go see to your son, I will wait here for you," Raisa's tone was soft, but firm.

Carolyn had lost the capacity to speak. She shook her head as if trying to wake up. She started getting up and, realizing she was naked, it all came flooding back to her. She was looking desperately for the robe she knew she'd had on last night.

"Here, Cara. Put this on."

Carolyn turned towards Raisa who handed her the white terry cloth robe. "Hurry back," Raisa smiled.

Carolyn almost ran to the door. She stopped in front of it, took a deep breath and went out to Simon.

****

Raisa lay in bed waiting for her. *Another morning after,* Raisa thought to herself, but this time she was the one left in bed. She could hear Carolyn's voice, soft and loving, calming Simon outside the room and she became captivated with all the affection she heard in it. Carolyn loved her son. It was obvious from the way she spoke to him.

She had known Carolyn almost two years to the day. And yet she realized she knew nothing about her. Not really. She knew all the factual details, of course, but she did not know Carolyn herself. Quite suddenly she was filled with a desire to know the woman whose body she had possessed a few hours ago. And the thought of that made Raisa remember.

Carolyn had been so passionate and responsive; it was as if her desire had been as great as Raisa's own. Raisa closed her eyes and was flooded with visions of Carolyn with her head thrown back, begging her not to stop. Carolyn's intake of breath the first time she had entered her. Raisa felt the desire fill every part of her body yet again. *How could this hunger still be unquenched?* She asked herself. She wanted Carolyn now more than ever.

Carolyn had not been merely a tool for her to take pleasure from; she had been a passionate participant. Carolyn had given her more pleasure than she had ever experienced before. And now, the morning after, she still wanted more; for the first time Raisa was in no hurry to leave.

She got up, walked towards the wide widow and pulled the curtain open. The sunlight came flooding in. The storm had finally passed and the sun was already making its appearance.

And that is how Carolyn saw her as she entered the room. She saw Raisa bathed in golden sunlight as it bounced off her perfectly sculptured body. Carolyn stood and stared for a mere second before she was able to speak to the woman who stood in front of her with an invitation that, although unspoken, was understood by both. *Come!*

"I think you should go," she said softly. Carolyn was caught between fear and an irrational need to run into those arms once again. She closed her eyes for a moment trying to control her shaking. When she opened them again Raisa stood in front of her with the glow of the sunlight shining behind her.

"I'm hungry too," Raisa said softly as she took Carolyn into her arms and took her mouth.

Carolyn began to respond, and then suddenly she pushed Raisa away as if she had been burned by her. "No, you have to go!"

"I need to touch you."

"No! And this is not the time to discuss this. You have to go," Carolyn insisted

"There is nothing to discuss. My body still needs you." Raisa reached for her again.

"Don't touch me! I want you to leave!" Carolyn spat out.

Raisa stood frozen in front of her. She was being dismissed and she acted the only way she knew how. She lashed back.

"I leave when I am good and ready. And I want you." She tried taking Carolyn into her arms yet again.

"Simon... Simon might hear you. Please, Raisa. Go...please."

"I want to see you later today then." Raisa still held tightly to Carolyn.

Carolyn pulled away and took a few steps away from her. "This was a mistake. A big mistake; I was frightened and I...."

"And you didn't know what you were doing?" Raisa finished for her sarcastically.

Carolyn stared at her. "Yes."

"Which time? Which time were you not sure it was what you wanted? The second or the fourth time we fucked?" Raisa's voice was filled with venom.

Carolyn closed her eyes and opened them again. Raisa rushed her and pinned her against the closest wall. Carolyn was shocked for a moment before she gasped when she felt Raisa's hand between her legs. Their faces were so close that she could feel Raisa's breath against her mouth as she spoke.

"You are still wet from having fucked with me. You can still feel my fingers inside you. I know that. I see it in your eyes. Or is it my mouth that you remember, Cara?" She finished saying in a soft accusation. "Your body is getting wet again. Can you feel it, Cara?" Raisa asked, as her fingers began slowly to caress the softness between Carolyn's legs.

"Raisa, please.... Please go. Simon," Carolyn said in barely a whisper. "Please." Carolyn begged as her eyes closed with newfound desire.

"Hide behind your son if you want to. But we both know that you enjoyed it. And remember, Cara mia, you fucked me back."

Raisa roughly released her.

Carolyn stood leaning against the wall as Raisa started picking up her clothes and dressing. When she was done she faced Carolyn once more. She stared at Carolyn for a moment and then walked out.

****

Raisa walked out of the bedroom and came face to face with Simon. He extended his hand to her and she, as if in a trance, took it.

"Hello. I'm Simon," he said with a smile.

"Hello Simon, I'm…"

"You are Ms. Andieta, my Mommy told me." He sounded very proud of himself for having all this knowledge. "You work with my Dad and you came to make sure we were okay."

Raisa could not help but smile. She usually found children bothersome; but she found herself reacting to the charming little boy with the bright smile and the innocent blue eyes. It was quite obvious that he was Carolyn's child. He also had the sunlight in his hair like his mother and the softness of her eyes.

"Are you going to have breakfast with us?" He asked just as Carolyn was coming out of the bedroom.

"Well, I am hungry," Raisa replied, turning back and giving Carolyn a smile, daring her to object.

"Simon darling, Ms. Andieta is a very busy person. Don't impose on her." Carolyn hoped that Raisa would take the hint.

"But, Mommy, she's hungry."

"Yes, I'm hungry," Raisa echoed with a devilish smile. The insinuation was not lost on Carolyn. She looked from Raisa to her son then back to Raisa.

"Then, of course, she must stay. Shall we order then?" Carolyn walked over to the telephone, trying to put some distance between Raisa and herself.

The three had breakfasted together. Raisa almost totally

ignored Carolyn. She engaged Simon in conversation and the boy was eating up all the attention. Raisa was really listening and Simon was quite animated. They laughed and giggled all throughout breakfast. Carolyn had a chance to see this woman in front of her from a whole new viewpoint. Raisa had just slid into this very intimate part of her life and she couldn't understand how it had all suddenly come about.

The world was spinning so fast she hadn't been able to catch her breath yet. And, as she was daydreaming, her eyes became fixed on Raisa's hands.

A soft moan escaped Carolyn's lips without her even realizing it. Her mind was filled with visions of what those hands had done. Those hands had caressed, teased and made her body soar over and over again. The same feeling of dizziness that she had experienced in Raisa's office was spreading through her body again and again the world began to spin.

She felt Raisa's hands on hers before she actually saw them. And when she looked up to meet those eyes she remembered how they changed when they were filled with passion. Raisa's voice broke through the haze.

"Are you dizzy, Cara?" Raisa kneeled next to her.

"Mommy, are you okay?"

Carolyn swallowed, broke eye contact with Raisa and directed her comments to Simon as she tried to catch her breath. "Yes, darling, I'm fine, just a little tired." She suddenly realized what she had said and looked at Raisa. They had hardly slept.

"You must lie down and get some rest," Raisa said softly.

"No!" Carolyn said much too quickly and pulled her hand away from Raisa's.

Raisa smiled and stood up. "Of course you must. Go lie down and I will have my car outside pick up your maid. While you are resting, I will keep Simon entertained until she arrives."

"No, you have done enough," Carolyn replied.

"Not enough, Cara, I wish I could do more," Raisa said with double meaning, sealing it with a smile filled with a promise. "Is this plan all right with you, Simon?" Raisa looked for an ally. She did not have to wait long.

"Mommy, come on. I will tuck you in. You look really

tired." Simon took his mother's hand and started walking her towards the bedroom.

"Simon, Ms. Andieta has been very kind but she is a very busy woman. We can look after ourselves. We mustn't impose." Carolyn tried desperately to get control of the situation.

"Nonsense Carolyn, I am doing this because I want to. Now go to bed. My driver shall bring back your maid to take care of things. I have some things to take care of in my office and tonight I shall come back and take you both home." Raisa picked up the phone and started putting her plan into action.

Simon tugged at his mother's sleeve and she allowed him to walk her to bed. *What have I gotten into?* Carolyn kept asking herself, over and over again.

Simon tucked her in and kissed her on the forehead before he walked out and closed the door behind him.

Carolyn kept going over things in her mind. How had this happened? How had she allowed it to happen? And now, how could she deal with Raisa Andieta? Raisa had made it perfectly clear that she had been taken. *How dare she assume that she could just take over things?* Carolyn thought to herself. *If Raisa Andieta thinks that she somehow now has some kind of right to force herself into my life, she will have another think coming! I'll be damned if I get within 20 feet of that woman ever again!* That was the last thought that Carolyn had before the weight of what she had lived through the last 24 hours took her into a sound sleep.

****

Raisa had waited for Clara to come and take over the care of Simon. Before she left she checked in on Carolyn and found her in a deep sleep. She stood before the sleeping woman for a moment, then walked out.

Raisa went home to shower and change. She called into her office and went over some things on the telephone as she was being driven to the office. There was a message from Matt Stenbeck. He had called to confirm his appointment and would be there by the time she arrived.

Raisa leaned back into the soft leather of the car. She would be meeting with the husband of the woman she had spent the night with. And although it was not the first time that she had slept with her executives' wife, this time it bothered her. It was not that she felt remorse or shame of having taken another man's wife. And it wasn't that she had any regrets. On the contrary, she wanted Carolyn now more than ever. What began to bother her was the thought that Carolyn was his wife. He had touched her and he would touch her again. At that thought, Raisa shook her head.

"What the hell is wrong with me?" She asked out loud.

"Ms. Andieta?" The driver asked.

"Just drive!" She yelled and stared out the limousine window without saying a word for the remainder of the drive.

Chapter Seven

Raisa walked into the Copeco Oil Headquarters building with all her energy.   She was on top.   That was all that had ever mattered.   She was in control and everyone knew it as they stepped aside as they saw her coming.   As she approached her office, she immediately saw Matt Stenbeck.

When he saw her approaching, he stood up to greet her.

"Ms. Andieta," he acknowledged.   She nodded in response.

"Come with me," was all she said and he followed her into her private office.   She walked around her desk and sat down.   "Sit down."

Matt sat quickly.   He had come straight to her office.   He had been trying to call his house and had received no answer.

"Mr. Stenbeck, what happened out at my rig?"   Raisa jumped right in.

"It seems that it was a deliberate explosion.   We found remnants of a small device.   We are still investigating."

"Did you get rid of Curbelo?"

"I have not been able to find him.   I did hear about his family."

"Yes, most unfortunate.   Have you notified the authorities?"   Raisa wanted to keep it all sterile.   She had learned early on that feeling was a weakness.   Compassion was a flaw that had no place in business.   Her father had taught her well.   She was a daughter, not the son he had wanted, but he had been proud at how easily she learned. He had once said that she was more of a man than anyone he had ever known and that he was proud of her ability to run his company.

Raisa had always wanted his approval. Her brother, Andreas, was weak in her father's eyes. All Andreas wanted to do was run the ranch. He was happy just tending the land. Martin Andieta had tried everything to get his son to toughen up, as he put it, but Andreas had remained steadfast in his convictions.

Then, it seemed, one day Martin Andieta noticed his daughter. He had been aware of her sharp intelligence and her desire to excel. Then quite unexpectedly he saw her desire to please him and please him she did. She became the best at everything. He taught her all that was important to him. He taught her how to shoot and ride a horse without fear. He taught her the desire to conquer and to vanquish. He taught her how to control and manipulate people. He taught her to be the heir he wanted to keep his empire intact and growing.

Mostly, he taught her not to need. And before he died he had looked at his creation with pride. She was truly all and more than he could have hoped for. She was self-sufficient. He had made her a fortress of strength. He had taught her the ability to be alone.

This is the woman who was facing Matt Stenbeck. She wanted the facts and none of the details that she found unnecessary. Matt was no lightweight, but even he found her disinterest at the loss of human casualties surprising.

"I have not been able to get in touch with the police... "He was interrupted.

"Good, we will take over. This business is out of your hands now. Give Estes all the details and get back out to the rig. I want security tight, Mr. Stenbeck. I don't want the flow to slow down anymore than it has already." She said all of this without a blink of an eye. "Have you made arrangements to replace the personnel you lost?" When she received no answer she looked up from the papers she was looking at.

"Ah...no, we will need a few days to bring them in from other rigs. It will slow us down a bit but it will be worth the security measure rather than just bringing in unscreened personnel." Matt watched as she sat back, now staring at him.

"Very good," she said, acknowledging his foresight. "I want you back out there today." She did not give him any other option.

"I will be going back in a few hours. I have had no word of my wife and son. I want to make sure that they are all right before I go back. I have everything bottled up at the rig."

"Your family is fine. They are now at the Caracas Hilton. It seems that they were caught out at the Autopista when the flooding took place. I had breakfast with them this morning."

"That answers why I couldn't get in touch with them." He smiled his thanks. "Carolyn tends to overreact sometimes. I wanted to make sure that all was well."

Raisa felt herself swallow down her disgust as she faced the man in front of her with dispassionate disinterest. "She had a right to be frightened, Mr. Stenbeck. She saw the water rising with her son in the car as others were submerged and drowned," Raisa said condescendingly.

"Of course she did. Of course she did. I want to thank you, Ms. Andieta, for all the trouble that you've taken with my family." He tried to make amends for his apparent lack of sensitivity.

"No trouble, Mr. Stenbeck. I found your son quite charming. Your wife and son are fine. I expect you out on the rig immediately." Again, she left him no other options.

"I figured I would be needed back. I have arranged for transportation back this evening. I will be picked up at home. So if there is nothing else you wish to know, I will give Mr. Estes all the details, updates and go to the hotel and take my wife and son home." Matt rose and Raisa nodded her dismissal. There was nothing else she could say.

She sat and looked at the door he shut as he left her office. *His wife... his wife...his wife.* How many times had he said that? She stood up and walked up to the glass wall that put the city of Caracas at her feet. *His wife.*

****

When Carolyn heard the buzzing from the door of the suite she looked up in dread and anticipation. Raisa had said she would be taking them home. She chastised herself and looked in the direction of the door as Clara went to answer it.

Carolyn had taken care when she dressed and lightly put some make up on. She had brushed her hair and now she looked more herself. She had had enough rest so that she could handle Raisa Andieta.

When the door opened she took a deep breath. Matt waltzed in, to her surprise, and Simon ran into his father's arms.

****

"Is Ms. Andieta available?" A police sergeant asked Gloria Bertran, Raisa's private secretary.

"Do you have an appointment?"

"She is expecting me. My name is Sargento Ramiro Fonseca."

Gloria looked at him suspiciously and picked up Raisa's private line.

"Ms. Andieta, I have a Sargento Fonseca that says…"

"Send him in," was all her boss said before Gloria was disconnected.

"Sargento, if you will please go through that door."

The sergeant nodded and disappeared into Raisa's private office.

****

Raisa did not speak to Carolyn that night. She did not communicate with her either. But from that day on she knew where Carolyn was every moment of the day and night.

As the city started settling after the disastrous landslides and

36

searching for the missing, the disturbances began again.   There were demonstrations and riots all over the city.   The populace was unhappy with how the government had handled the emergencies. There had been very little in terms of relief and the death count was still growing due to the unsanitary conditions now created by stagnant water. Cholera was making its ugly face visible among the poor.

Disease ran through the barrios and left death and more despair in its path.   The University students began their protest marches and the army was called in to put down the civil unrest. The military began to be more visible.   And the arrests and interrogations of known activists began to take its toll. The city of Caracas was becoming a powder keg that was going to explode at any moment.

Elected officials began to fear the motorcycles since they seemed to be a very viable way of being shot at with the shooter escaping quickly.   Security was tightened.   The anger and frustration became a palatable entity.

Chapter Eight

"Raisa, I cannot give you any more security!"

"Carlos, I have paid dearly for things like this not to happen!"

"Raisa, calm down. You know that I count on your support and friendship. I promise you that this will not be left without justice being exacted."

"Mr. President, I am losing 20,000 barrels of oil on a daily basis. Don't tell me you are doing your best!"

"Raisa, I will give you military protection."

"I don't want military protection. My rigs are mine. I don't want soldiers near them. Don't play this game with me because I will hit you with everything I have in my power," she threatened.

"No, my friend. That was a sincere offer of assistance," Presidente Carlos Arturo Padron reassured her in his most diplomatic demeanor.

"I'm sure it was, Mr. President. Thank you, but no. I don't require military intervention."

"Very well then. I shall stay in touch and count on your friendship." He waited for her assurance.

"Of course, Mr. President. You have my friendship." With the reassurance of support given, she hung up the phone. *That son of a bitch. I am going to enjoy burying him,* she thought to herself. *His days are numbered.*

****

Demonstrations started erupting at the least expected times. Civil unrest was becoming felt even at the highest level. Security had become paramount in all public and private events. Copeco was hosting a fund-raiser for the Bolivar Museum and armed guards were present to assure nothing unwanted would occur. All Copeco executives were expected to attend.

Raisa, who normally hated these occasions, was expectant and nervous. She had been more focused in some ways, and more in control than ever. She had managed to keep herself focused on a goal. The world around her was going to change and she was adamant about being one of the catalysts. She was the queen and her entourage buzzed around her. She ruled over them all with a sense of confidence until she saw, from the corner of her eye, Matt and Carolyn Stenbeck enter the ballroom.

Matt had his arm possessively around his wife's waist. That was when the control began to slip away from Raisa's armor. She followed their entrance as they went from person to person with their hellos.

Raisa took in every part of Carolyn's body and the heat she thought she had control of within her became a roaring fire once more. Almost on cue, Carolyn looked in her direction as if sensing the primal call and their eyes fused. Carolyn stared back with the same hunger.

Almost as if willed to, Carolyn separated herself from Matt and walked towards her. Raisa never looked away. Then, quite suddenly, Carolyn stood before her.

"I need to talk to you," Carolyn said softly in almost a whisper.

"Yes," was all that would come out of Raisa's lips. "Come with me." Carolyn followed her.

They walked through a door and into an office. Raisa was unable to move as Carolyn walked slowly up to her. "What mischief have you been up to lately?" Carolyn said as a finger traced Raisa's jaw slowly.

Raisa began to realize that she was loosing control and was about to speak when Carolyn put her finger on her lips. The touch became an anesthetic. Raisa's breathing became audible. Her head fell back as her body leaned onto the desk behind her. Carolyn's mouth found her neck and her hands began to explore Raisa's body.

"Carolyn, oh God, Cara mia, touch me…"

Their lovemaking was rushed with need. Their hunger was something that needed quenching quickly. Both women touched, bit, kissed, caressed and received pleasure from one another.

They had ended up on a couch completely naked. Carolyn lay on her back and Raisa on her side with her face resting on Carolyn's breasts. Her hand was possessively holding Carolyn's thigh. Carolyn suddenly began to stroke Raisa's hair and the other woman kissed the breast she laid on, resting her face again on its softness.

Both women had been careful not to look directly at each other after their bodies had been sated. They were fused together by the most delicate of string and each just wanted to enjoy what was left of the moment and the pleasure without having to face what they had done.

Raisa looked up sharply as she heard the jiggling of the doorknob and made out what was being said on the other side of the door. She rose quickly looking down on Carolyn for a mere instant. Carolyn stared in horror at the door. Raisa looked around, grabbed the dress that lay closest to her on the floor and put it over Carolyn. The door burst open before she was able to turn completely.

"Que esta pasando aqui?" A very irate gentleman, followed by a bus boy, went mute as soon as he took in the scene in front of him.

Carolyn turned her face away as she tried to cover her body. Raisa stood to her full height and faced the man without even a blink of nervousness.

"Tu! Eres el gerente!" She demanded to know if he was the manager. The man nodded, unable to stop his staring. "Cierra esa puerta y controla tu perro. Te conpensare con mas dinero que has visto en toda tu vida." The gentlemen nodded his agreement and complied with her request to control his dog, as she called it. He told the bus boy to wait outside and not say a word. She had offered him more money than he would ever see in his lifetime. The manager recognized the authority in her bearing. Instantly, he knew

41

she was not a woman to cross.

Raisa motioned him to turn around. He complied. She quickly knelt down next to Carolyn. "It's all right. It's going to be all right." Her voice was soft and gentle. "No one saw anything here; I promise you that." Raisa tried to reassure her, but Carolyn looked at her with fear-filled eyes.

Carolyn stared as Raisa walked over to the man and spoke to him. She had not bothered to put one stitch of clothing on. She defied all sense of reason and challenged anyone to defy her with her bravado. Carolyn saw the man nod and walk out the door without looking back.

Carolyn rose and began to dress as quickly as possible. Raisa just stood and stared at her without saying a word. When Carolyn was finished she finally looked up and met Raisa's stare.

"What now?" Raisa asked looking defiantly at her.

Carolyn looked away and found no point of reference. Raisa waited until her own impatience showed itself. Suddenly there was an ocean between them.

"Did I take advantage of the situation this time, Cara?" Raisa asked sarcastically.

"You are a pig!" Carolyn spat as she started walking towards the door. Raisa reached for her and pulled her towards her.

"Was this a mistake too?" Raisa demanded not releasing her.

"An experiment." Carolyn's comment hit Raisa harder than if her face had been slapped.

Raisa quickly released her. Both women stood challenging one another.

"I see… well…now that we have established the parameters," Raisa said as her eyes became like dark chips of anger.

"What are you talking about? This will not happen again." Carolyn spoke with superiority.

"Won't it?" Raisa gave her a malevolent smile.

"No, it won't," Carolyn assured her.

"How much?"

Carolyn stared, suddenly understanding what the insinuation was. "You are disgusting! I am not a prostitute!"

"We have established the parameters, Cara mia. We are

merely discussing terms," Raisa said to her, quite seriously, as she reached out to take Carolyn's breast.

Carolyn went at her. Raisa grabbed both her hands and in the struggle they both fell onto the floor. They rolled like two cats fighting for dominance.

"Get off me!" Carolyn demanded furiously as Raisa pinned her.

"No money then?" Raisa mocked her. Carolyn struggled beneath her. "Oh, now I really understand. You do it just because you like it." Raisa's tone was even more mocking. Raisa's mouth covered her savagely and her hand went between Carolyn's legs.

When Raisa released one hand to touch the woman beneath her she was struck across the face hard. Raisa struck her back, and again pinned her down, kissing her until they could both taste blood. Raisa pulled away and her eyes looked into a mirror of her own emotions in Carolyn's eyes. She needed to touch her, kiss her, taste her and be one with her again. They stared at one another as their bodies started the primal dance once more.

"I'm sorry," Raisa said meaningfully, but in a whisper. As Raisa searched Carolyn's eyes and as they closed, Carolyn offered her neck and her hunger. Raisa kissed the delicate neck before her.

A moan escaped Carolyn's mouth as her hand pulled Raisa closer to her. Raisa's mouth traveled to capture the lips that beckoned. As both mouths met, Carolyn opened hers. She needed the connection too. The kiss that followed was softer and the hands that had fought one another pulled and tugged. Once again they gave into the passion that always rose within them. Their bodies rubbed against one another and pleasure once again was given and taken.

After the panting and the breathing began to slow, they both got up and started dressing. Neither said a word and neither looked at the other. Neither spoke as they checked their appearance in the mirror in the side bathroom and then walked out. It was as if they had both chosen not to acknowledge what had just transpired between them. Each women had lost and won and, for now, that was enough.

As they entered the ballroom again, Carolyn gave Raisa a side-glance as she spotted Matt and headed toward him. Raisa did not have to hide her eyes now. She watched as Carolyn walked back to her husband. She watched as he leaned down and said something in her ear. Raisa felt her face flush with heat. Her eyes closed as memories of how Carolyn had felt beneath her threatened her sanity. She turned and walked away, as far from Carolyn as possible. She couldn't stand by and watch Matt pawing what was, in her mind, hers.

For the rest of the evening, their eyes sought each other. At one point Raisa stared, not caring who noticed. Matt kept rubbing Carolyn's back. The touch being symbolic that she was his wife. Raisa began to breathe harder as she began to feel her rage building. She chastised herself for getting so out of control with a woman who was not hers and hers alone. This was something she was not used to. She would stop this situation with Carolyn Stenbeck; she had other things to think about. In her mind, this affair was over. She finally turned around and walked out the party without once looking back.

Carolyn watched as Raisa left and she also told herself it was all over.

Chapter Nine

The death count from the rains was devastating. Civil unrest could be felt in the air. There was talk of a workers' strike and the army was now in a full 24-hour alert status. Graffiti, which was always present, began to take a political tinge. Flyers started to appear at universities and fly-by-night newspapers were being spread to the populace.

President Padron was escalating security around La Casa Rosada, the official presidential residence. There was an obvious military presence everywhere. Terror escalated and the number of victims began to rise.

****

"Matt, I want to leave Caracas!"

"Carolyn, you are over reacting, as usual!"

"Am I, Matt? Look around you. I want to take Simon back home for awhile."

"No! He is my son too, Carolyn. You are not taking him anywhere." Matt began to pace.

Carolyn knew that this was not the way to approach Matt.

With the laws of the country being what they were, she needed Matt's permission to be able to take Simon out of the country. She needed to stay focused and do whatever she must. For the first time since she had moved to Venezuela she was truly afraid.

When she drove to the market she could see the parking lot secured by the army. There was an over abundance of a police presence, which everyone knew was yet another corrupt organization. Sides were clearly being established.

****

The protests at the universities began suddenly and in great numbers. The students took to the streets. The army rolled. Chaos followed, electricity was interrupted and the city of lights became a city of violence. El Carolazo, they called it. In all the barrios, people opened their windows and started banging pots and pans loudly. The roar was deafening. The populace was not happy and like a sleeping giant it had begun to roar. The army moved in. Some demonstrators were taken in for questioning. The air became heavy; it was all a matter of time before civil war would erupt.

****

A month later the argument was still the same but Carolyn was even more stressed. She lived in constant fear that one day she might be faced with a situation that she would not be able to control and she and Simon would be alone to face it.

"Matt, please, let me take Simon to the states for awhile."

"No!"

"Matt, you won't even be here. You're going to be out in the oilrigs and if anything happens we will be cut off from each other for who knows how long. Let me take him to visit my parents for just awhile. He is out of school now in any case. Please, Matt." She hoped that he would see the logic of her argument.

"Carolyn, we live in a very secure area…"

"Secure? Nothing is secure, Matt. There are soldiers with machine guns in the supermarket parking lots and on the street. If anything breaks out they are not going to care where we live. No one will be safe, and you won't be here!" Carolyn cried hysterically.

"Carolyn…" he began when Clara came into the room.

"Mr. Stenbeck, Ms. Andieta in on the phone and wishes to speak to you. Shall I tell her you are at home?"

"Of course I am home for Ms. Andieta. I'll take the call in here." Matt walked over to the small table and picked up the receiver. "Hello Ms. Andieta."

Carolyn's arms went around her body protectively. She had managed to stop thinking of Raisa. And now, when she had thought that she had gotten her out of her system, her presence was making itself known. Carolyn turned her back to Matt. She had to think of how to get Simon out of Venezuela. She kept telling herself they were all blind. The unrest could be felt on the street. No matter how hard Padron would try to control the students, they still protested and, sooner or later, the bolder ones would pull the first trigger. She had to get her son out of this violent land. She would do it whether Matt liked it or not. She would find a way.

She was so deeply in thought that when two arms pulled her back into an embrace she jumped in fear. She turned quickly and found herself staring at an angered face.

"What has gotten into you?" Matt tried grabbing her again. "I just wanted to hold you."

"Don't," Carolyn said as she put some distance between them.

"How long is this going to go on, Carolyn? You are my wife. I have tried to be patient with you," he reasoned as he started to approach her.

"I don't feel well, Matt." She avoided looking into his eyes.

"You haven't felt well in a long time, Carolyn. If you think that I am going become a monk, you are very much mistaken. You better be feeling better by tonight!" He slammed the door on his way out.

47

Matt called her later from the office. Apparently some of the directors had been invited for a week to the Hacienda Virago deep in the interior of the country. Ms. Andieta rarely invited people out to the hacienda and this was not an invitation that was to be turned down. As soon as Carolyn hung up the phone she closed her eyes and leaned her head against the wall. They were both coming in for the kill; Matt and Raisa were takers. She would be damned if she were to become the meat to feed them.

She hated this land. She understood it less and less each day. The violence somehow permeated everything with its raw sensuality. Everything was too exposed. She was too exposed.

Carolyn had not slept with Matt since that first time she had been with Raisa. The thought of hands, any hands, touching her made her stomach turn after that first time with Raisa. She had not been able to stand even the thought of being touched. Until it became all she thought about. She would wake up in the middle of the night drenched in perspiration as she dreamed of hands touching her body and just at the moment when she would surrender, a face would fill her vision, and it was that of Raisa Andieta. It got to the point where she avoided being in the same building with her.

And then of course it happened. That night at the Copeco Ball she had told herself over and over again that she could handle it. She had looked around and had actually managed to act the way that Matt had always wanted her to. In other words, acted the part. She was talking to Consuelo Betancourt, one of the very few female executives at Copeco, when quite suddenly she heard a voice call to her. *Look at me.* Her eyes almost knew instinctively and she looked straight into the eyes of Raisa Andieta.

Her body heard the call and she was unable to stop herself. She walked up to Raisa, nothing else mattered but the fact that her blood was rumbling through her veins, and the pounding in her ears was threatening to deafen her. She saw her hand reach out for Raisa and was surprised when the words 'I need to talk to you,' came out of her mouth. Raisa had simply said, 'Yes, come with me,' and she had followed.

Both knew what the other one wanted. For the first time in her life Carolyn had acted out of pure instinct. Now it seemed she would pay for that mistake for the rest of her life.

Chapter Ten

"Andreas, I want you there. Tell Nona that I will be arriving in a day or two." Raisa's voice was melodic as she spoke to her brother. "I know that things are questionable right now but our position is solid. Don't worry about that."

She was interrupted by a knock on the door, followed by Gloria, her secretary, entering her office.

"Andreas, wait a moment, will you?" Raisa then covered the phone and addressed Gloria. "Why are you interrupting me, Gloria?"

"Ms. Andieta, it's Carolyn Stenbeck on line two. I thought that.... I can tell her you will call her back." Gloria was unsure and afraid of her boss's temper. She remembered how Raisa had despaired over this woman before and she also knew that she was still employed because she knew the meaning of discretion.

"No, no... I'll take the call. Thank you, Gloria." Raisa removed her hand from the telephone. "Andreas, I will have to call you back later. Asta pronto." She pressed the button of the number two line before taking a deep breath.

"Carolyn..." her voice had come out huskier than she had intended. She only heard silence but she knew that Carolyn was listening.

"Raisa.... I am going to ask you for something and I want you to say yes."

Raisa laughed out loud, taken off guard. This she had not

expected. "What do you want?" She asked, still in good spirits.

"I want to leave Venezuela and I need your help to take my son with me."

There was silence for a minute before Raisa spoke. "I gather Matt doesn't see things your way." It was a statement, not a question.

"No, he does not." Raisa could hear the slight twinge of stress in her voice. This call had cost her dearly.

"Are you leaving him?" She was brutally direct.

"No, I am taking Simon home. I'm afraid for his safety here."

"Liar."

"Is that your answer?"

"No, it's not."

Again the silence stood between them.

"I will do anything," Carolyn said suddenly.

"Cara, I haven't asked for anything," she answered sarcastically.

"Are you going to help me or not?" Carolyn demanded.

"I have invited a few families to the country…" Raisa spoke as if she had not heard the question until she was quickly interrupted in mid sentence.

"Raisa, I can't wait that long," Carolyn said sharply.

"It's only a few days, Carolyn," Raisa bit back.

"I know you can do this if you want. It has to be right away." The stress was beginning to show in Carolyn's voice again.

"All right, when you come to the hacienda in two days I will…"

"I want to go today, now!" Raisa could now hear the touch of hysteria in Carolyn's voice.

"What's wrong, Carolyn? What's going on?" Raisa demanded. The line went dead. Carolyn had hung up.

Raisa stared at the phone in disbelief, and tried calling her back several times but the phone was not being picked up. She called down for her car to be brought around and she left the office.

****

Clara ran to the door as quickly as she could. The knocking was persistent. She opened the door and was pushed aside.

"Where is Mrs. Stenbeck?" Raisa demanded.

Clara was about to speak when she saw two men enter the house dressed in dark suits and the question she was about to ask died in her throat.

"Where is she?" Raisa demanded again.

Clara, terrified, pointed to the staircase.

Raisa looked at the two men as if a message was given and understood. She then turned and went up the flight of stairs. She opened door upon door until she was faced with Carolyn. There were two suitcases on the bed and clothes thrown everywhere.

Something had happened, Raisa could feel that something had happened and it was about to shift everything in her life.

"Why the rush?" Raisa tried to sound unconcerned.

"How did you...." Carolyn began to ask, but the question died in her mouth as she added, "like everything else you just pushed in, didn't you?"

"I've had no complaints, Cara," Raisa answered with a smile.

"Just get out! I don't need your help. I will pay off whoever. After all, everything is for sale, isn't it?" Carolyn began to throw clothes in the suitcases again.

Raisa was about to give her a flippant remark when she noticed Carolyn's eyes were about to overflow with tears. She took a few steps away and looked around the room. When she spoke again her voice held no sarcasm. "Why the rush?"

"This is not new. I have wanted to leave for a long time." Carolyn continued to pack.

"Why right now? I told you in two days..."

"I can't wait two days!" Carolyn faced her again.

"I swear you Americans are insane. I don't know why I bother with Americanas like you!" Raisa said in disdain. She barely had enough time to move before Carolyn threw something at her.

51

"You almost hit my face, you bitch!"

Carolyn grabbed another shoe and, was about to throw it, when Raisa tackled her onto the bed.

A loud roar was heard in the distance. At the sound Carolyn began to whimper. Raisa just looked down at the woman beneath her in surprise. The thunder was heard even closer this time and Carolyn hid her face in Raisa's embrace.

"It's all right, Cara," Raisa began to say softly as her mouth placed light kisses on her forehead, beginning its search.

"Get off me!" Demanded Carolyn suddenly.

"Calm down."

"This is his bed! Get off me!"

Raisa got up and Carolyn got off as if the sheets had burned her. All of a sudden, reality hit hard. This was Carolyn's bed. She stared at it unable to look away.

Both Raisa and Carolyn heard as the winds began to pick up and the rain started coming down hard. The noise of the raindrops as they hit the roof filled their ears and after awhile the roar of the thunder and the harshness of the storm assaulting the roof was all that she could hear and feel.

The next crash of thunder hid the primal scream that came out of Raisa as she started pulling everything off the bed. The electricity went out suddenly and Carolyn just stared, unable to stop her or aid her. Raisa had thrown everything on the floor and torn at the sheets until the bed lay bare. She was breathing hard like it had not been enough. She then turned her eyes towards Carolyn.

Her Carolyn! His wife! His bed! She screamed like an animal does when in pain. She started tearing at whatever she could grab. Her pain became anger. And to Raisa Andieta anger always equaled violence. Control was all she knew, all that kept her world intact and in control was the last thing she felt at that moment.

"Does he touch you better than me?" Raisa asked in what seemed barely a whisper. "Is the pleasure with him what you want!" She screamed now as she kept the distance that separated her from Carolyn.

Carolyn started to break the status quo as she moved slightly towards her, her hand reaching for her slowly. When her hand was about to reach Raisa's face it was slapped away.

Suddenly, Raisa pushed Carolyn against the wall and held her there with her own body.

"How did he touch you, Cara? Tell me! Tell me!" Raisa was screaming. "I can do anything better than him! Tell me! How did he touch you!" Raisa was totally out of control now.

"I want you," Carolyn said between tears softly.

"Arrgghhh...." Raisa hit the wall behind her with a cry of anger and despair.

Carolyn tried kissing her but she turned her face away. Raisa however still held her, not releasing her hold. Carolyn buried her face in Raisa neck. "I haven't been with him since the first time I was with you." Carolyn heard a moan of shear anguish as Raisa began to sob and she held her tighter.

Carolyn had held on. Raisa at first tried to push herself away. When Carolyn held onto her even tighter she seemed to just surrender, her arms going around Carolyn desperately.

Raisa's rage and sobs continued as Carolyn held her, crying as well. An hour, a lifetime, forever. There was only that moment. They slid down the wall and as the sobs and the anger subsided all that could be heard was the storm still raging inside and outside the bedroom that enclosed them.

Carolyn held Raisa to her with her back against the wall as they both lay on the floor. Time had just seemed to stop for them. Raisa was half lying on her, as her face lay on Carolyn's chest. Carolyn began to softly caress her hair and Raisa's eyes closed as her mouth turned up to meet the lips she knew were waiting.

The kiss was soft and tender. And when the mouths parted they remained close enough so that their breaths were but a whisper away in the darkness of the room.

"Come with me," Raisa begged.

"Yes."

Suddenly filled with strength, Raisa got up and offered Carolyn her hand. Carolyn saw her clearly as lightning lit the room and the lights came back on. She saw the hand extended to her and took it.

Silently, they both exited the room. Raisa held onto her hand tightly. They walked down the hallway untill Carolyn suddenly stopped and pulled away.

53

"Simon…. I can't leave him."

"Where is he?"

"At a friend's house."

"We will pick him up. Come," Raisa took Carolyn's hand possessively and led her down the staircase.

When they reached the foyer where the maid and her two men waited, Raisa stopped for only a moment.

"Rodolfo, take Mrs. Stenbeck into the car and wait for me."

Carolyn was about to say something, then seemed to change her mind just as quickly. Raisa was in control; she had surrendered it for now and simply followed instructions. She felt so tired.

"Tell Mr. Stenbeck that Mrs. Stenbeck and his son are with me at my ranch. I am Raisa Andieta, do you understand?"

"Yes, Ms. Andieta," answered the maid nervously. She knew better than to question people like Ms. Andieta. Nothing good ever came of it.

"Good," Raisa Andieta said as she left, followed by her other associate.

****

As soon as she got into the limousine she had been escorted to, she had entered a closed dome. A partition separated the passengers from the bodyguards. Raisa got in several minutes later and when the door was closed she took Carolyn into her arms protectively.

"Where is your son?"

They gave the driver the address and the car pulled out to retrieve its other passenger.

Chapter Eleven

The trip to the hacienda was in some ways a complete blur. Carolyn was emotionally drained. She remembered allowing Raisa to make all the decisions. They had picked up Simon and Raisa was the one to talk to him and keep him occupied while she seemed to be in a dormant state.

Raisa had made all the arrangements necessary from her car phone. They were taken to a small airfield where they boarded a private plane.

As they were settled, one of the attendants spoke to Simon about what he would like to eat. Raisa reached out and covered Carolyn's hand briefly, then picked up the ringing telephone again.

It suddenly occurred to Carolyn that she had been running away from one prison to another. Again, not of her own choosing. She had not stopped to think. And this time Simon would be affected. She had been so upset with Matt's threats, the growing, visible military presence in the country, that she had just lost perspective. She had fallen right into Raisa's arms again. *How had this happened?*

All her life Carolyn had thought things through. She had always weighed the consequences of her actions. But with Raisa Andieta it had all changed. Perhaps it was this land, with its violence and machismo that had thrown her off keel. All Carolyn knew was that she was confused and tired and, of course, there was Raisa. What would she do with the choice of Raisa now? Carolyn looked towards Simon and it all seemed surreal somehow. She closed her eyes and gave in to the sleep she so badly seemed to need.

****

As Raisa sat back and watched Carolyn sleep, she contemplated her actions. It would take a few hours to reach Hacienda Virago. She had never taken anyone home. That's what Virago was to her, home. All she loved was there. Yes, she had invited people over but never into her bed there. No one had ever mattered that much to her. With Carolyn she had not thought; it just seemed the natural thing to do.

There, of course, would be Nona to account to and her brother. But, she would have her way. She was Raisa Andieta and she wanted Carolyn in her house, in her bed and yes, she had to admit, she wanted Carolyn in her life. All these things came to her within the space of a second, rushing in, flooding her mind.

This was unfamiliar territory. Before she had always known how to proceed. She had always known what she wanted and how to get it. This was different somehow. Raisa closed her eyes as she remembered all the emotions that had gone through her back in the bedroom that Carolyn shared with her husband. She was filled with emotions foreign and new to her. All she had wanted was to destroy and tear apart. Raisa had always prided herself on her control. The hardest lesson she had learned, the one taught best to her by her father, was that to win one must control. And yet, she had no control over her feelings or her actions when it came to this woman sitting here beside her.

Raisa continued to stare at Carolyn as she slept. She recalled past lovers, and remembered her enjoyment of such affairs. She had always been in control with them all. Now, this woman had changed it all and she felt unsure and uncertain of every word and action. With Carolyn it had just happened, there was no conscious thought. Carolyn was something that was so deep inside her that she had become a part of her.

It then occurred to her that Nona knew nothing of her tastes, for lack of a better term. Nona had raised her. She had been more than a nanny. She was as close to a mother as Raisa had ever known. Her own mother had left them and gone back to Italy. Nona had stayed and loved her and Andreas. Her approval would be important. Raisa admitted for the first time, perhaps in a long time, that she would dread a look of disapproval from the old woman. But, Carolyn was not a choice. Carolyn was something she had to have.

Andreas was no innocent. He knew that Raisa took, as she wanted. He knew she took many and often. He had always just looked the other way and never said anything. She was his big sister and she had always protected him. Especially when their father had not been as understanding of his choices. Raisa had always stood by him. He would support her in everything.

Raisa shook her head, trying to keep the cobwebs from forming any further. She looked out the window and saw the greenery and the ocean of the country she so loved. Venezuela was her heart, wild and spoiled, yet innocent and uncertain, like a child going from childhood into the uncertain steps of adulthood. If she looked deeper within herself she would have to admit that, like Andreas, once upon a time she would have just loved never to leave Virago. But, unlike Andreas, she had let her heart be swayed by the desire to attain love from someone who, perhaps, did not deserve it.

She was tired of thinking. Simon had fallen asleep soon after Carolyn. She found herself staring at Carolyn again. Soon, they would be at Virago, she thought. How to proceed then?

****

They arrived at the hacienda after dark. Two black Explorers waited at the airstrip. They all got into the air-conditioned cabin and escaped the heat of the surrounding jungles. Carolyn did not utter a word. Simon half lay on her, still half asleep. In the darkness of the vehicle Carolyn felt Raisa's hand hold her own.

Carolyn simply laid her head on the shoulder of the woman next to her.

Raisa smiled into the darkness.

****

All were asleep in the hacienda when they arrived. A servant and Nona met them at the front portals. Raisa entered the house with her arm around an emotionally exhausted Carolyn, leading Simon by the hand.

Nona instantly took in the scene. She gave Raisa a smile immediately.

"Raisa," Nona said with such love in her voice.

"Nona," with a simple word she said it all. "Did they prepare the rooms next to mine for them?"

"Si, mi amor, todo esta preparado como tu pediste." It was all ready, as she had wished.

"Gracias, Nona." She smiled and guided both Carolyn and Simon to their rooms.

Nona watched as Raisa walked away with her arm protectively over the blonde woman and the fair-haired little boy. This was a different Raisa, she thought to herself. And she told herself that in time her little girl would come to her and tell her about it.

****

All Carolyn remembered of her first night at Virago was Raisa helping her with her clothes, the smell of clean sheets, then the soft arms that held her through the night.

****

Raisa woke up with the light of day.   She looked at the woman that lay half on top of her and leaned down, smelled her hair and, as she did, her arms tightened around the woman in her arms.

She had always woken alone whenever she was at Virago. Now that would change. Finally, she had all she wanted. She knew that as certainly as she knew she had Carolyn now here in her arms. Nothing would take what belonged to her from her. Nothing and no one would be allowed to. She would be ready for whatever came.

****

Carolyn woke up alone.   She missed something.   She was sure that Raisa had held her during the night. It had all become such a blur. She sat up in bed and looked to see she was naked under the sheets. Now she was sure Raisa had been there. She could still feel her arms around her body and the air was still filled with her perfume.

She noticed a pair of slacks and a blouse lying on the bed along with other essentials.   She could hear Simon's laughter coming from outside the window.   She wrapped the sheet around herself and walked to look outside.

Carolyn could see Simon laughing below in the courtyard. He sat in front of Raisa on a black powerful looking horse.   Raisa was also laughing.   There was no aloofness in her manner, only plain joy, which could be seen in her features. Carolyn watched from the window and listened.

"That was great, can we do it again please?" Simon begged with excitement.

"All right. Are you ready?" She was as excited as the boy was.

"Yes, please, I'm ready."

Carolyn stared as the black horse took off in a gallop, and she was terrified.   Suddenly, both horse and riders turned and headed back towards the house in a full gallop towards a fence. Carolyn's breathing seized.   The black horse flew over the fence with ease, but Carolyn felt the room close in on her as she could hardly breathe.

She ran out of the room, sheet and all.

Raisa and Simon were still laughing when she came face to face with them. Raisa smiled broadly as she took in Carolyn's attire.

"Are you crazy!" Carolyn shouted. She was furious.

Raisa became serious and Simon stopped smiling.

"How dare you endanger my son that way!"

"Mommy..." Simon tried to say.

"Get down from there, Simon! Get down from there this instant!"

Raisa helped the boy down from the horse without so much as a word.

"But, Mommy, it wasn't her fault. I asked her to jump," Simon said, trying to diffuse the situation.

"Simon, you are a boy. You don't know any better," she told him, then turned to Raisa who looked moodily at her in silence.

"How could you be so irresponsible!" Carolyn demanded. Raisa stared, saying nothing. She turned her horse and galloped away.

Carolyn just stared as she rode away. She stomped her foot in frustration and started walking back to the house with Simon in tow.

"Mommy, don't be mad at her, it was my fault!" The boy said, pouting.

An elderly looking lady waiting at the door interrupted the procession.

"Buenos dias," the woman said with a smile on her face.

"Oh, buenos dias." Carolyn realized that she had run out with only a sheet around herself. "I'm sorry, I don't speak Spanish very well."

"I will try to speak English," Nona said to her.

"Thank you." Carolyn smiled.

"You go and get dressed and I will bring you up your breakfast." Nona tried to hide the amusement of the sheet.

Carolyn looked down and smiled too. "Thank you."

60

****

Simon sat on her bed as she spoke to him from the bathroom.

"You have to use better judgment, Simon. You could have been killed!"

"Oh Mom…. Raisa's a great rider.   She won awards and everything for it," the boy tried to assure.

"How do you know all that?"

"She told me.   You should see all the things she can do on a horse," he said excitedly.

"Well, that might be true, but she should never have taken you for a jump like that."

"Oh Mom."

They were interrupted by a knock on the door.

"Come in," Carolyn said from the bathroom.

Carolyn stuck her head out and saw Nona with a tray. She immediately walked out and took it from her.

"Here, let me help you with that," Carolyn said as she set the tray down.

"I am Nona, Raisa's Nana."

Carolyn knew that this person had been important to Raisa and possibly could be still. "Please, won't you sit?"

Nona sat down with a smile.

"Mommy, can I go outside and play?"

"Yes. But Simon, no more adventures okay?"

"Okay, okay," the little boy said with a disappointed look on his face.

Carolyn sat and smelled the fresh coffee. "Mmmm… that smells wonderful, thank you. Won't you join me?"

"Yes, thank you."   Carolyn poured two cups.

"You are important to Raisa," the old woman stated bluntly and she noticed how the pot shook for a brief moment in Carolyn's hand as she poured the coffee.

"Am I?" She asked with a smile, avoiding eye contact.

61

"Yes, you are."

Carolyn continued to pour as she smiled.

"You reprimanded her and she said nothing to you. No one does that to my little girl and gets away with it," Nona said with a giggle as she took a sip of the coffee.

"I'm sorry. I was really frightened for Simon," Carolyn tried to explain.

"Oh, don't worry about it, my dear," Nona said as she patted Carolyn in the hand. "My Raisa is used to getting her own way and sometimes she gets carried away. But she is a good rider. Your boy was safe. However, she should have asked you. Not frightened you like that."

"I have never met anyone like her." Carolyn surprised herself by how honestly she spoke to the little woman in front of her.

"Yes, my Raisa is unique."

Carolyn smiled at the doting woman. *If you only knew,* she thought to herself. *This is the way it would always be if I were with Raisa. Never knowing what to expect.*

"You are like my Raisa, always thinking too hard."

"Yes, sometimes. But Raisa, she just seems to be able to fight the whole world and keep on going."

"It may seem that way. But she has a heart bigger than anyone I have ever known."

Carolyn looked at her for a moment and smiled with a nod. She wasn't sure if they were talking about the same woman. The Raisa she was used to was no softy. The Raisa she knew was temperamental and moody. She was egotistical, aggressive, and passionate to a fault. Yes, she knew all about Raisa's passion. She suddenly felt embarrassed and blushed as she looked up to meet the old woman's eyes.

"I know that she cares for you and your son very much," Nona said, trying to read the reactions on Carolyn's face.

"How can you tell?" Carolyn asked softly, looking down at her cup.

"Because she brought you here." Nona placed her hand over Carolyn's.

Carolyn looked up, smiled shyly and looked down again.

"She has invited people to Virago many times but they have never stayed in her private part of the Hacienda. That is how I know."

Carolyn got up quickly and set the cup down on the tray. She felt nervous, fear slipping in.

"Raisa is hard to know. But she is so much more than people see."

"Yes, she is. She is a world all to herself," Carolyn said distantly.

"Well Nona, have you told her all my secrets?" Raisa said half seriously, half teasing from the door.

Carolyn turned around and their eyes locked. Nona looked from one to the other. *They are like...* Nona thought. She was about to think they were like lovers facing each other, but, of course, that was not possible.

"Ah, Cara mia, come in and make up with your friend. I have things to do." Nona waved her into the room.

"I think she is mad at me, Nona," Raisa said to the old woman with a smile but her eyes said something differently.

"She will forgive you. Just promise to behave." The old woman went out of the room after patting Raisa on the face lovingly.

Raisa stood in front of Carolyn. She looked magnificent with her dark wind blown hair. Her face was flushed from the ride. With her blouse half-opened, white riding pants fitting snug to her body and high black riding boots she was the epitome of raw power and unbridled sensuality. Carolyn was suddenly filled with a hunger that shook her. She turned around and walked slowly to the window. At that moment she needed the distance in order to get her thoughts in order.

Raisa came up behind her until they barely touched. After a moment she spoke softly into Carolyn's ear. "I'm sorry I frightened you."

"You always frighten me," Carolyn said just as softly. "Your whole world frightens me."

Carolyn felt arms come from behind and pull her close until

she could feel Raisa's body as if it were her second skin. She could hear Raisa's breathing in her ear, and an ache began inside her. Carolyn moaned as her head went back onto Raisa's shoulder. Suddenly, she was quickly turned around. Her mouth was taken with the passion she feared, but could not stay away from.

"Raisa, wait…" she said between the onslaught.

"No, I need you now." And with that all words were silenced.

Carolyn tasted the saltiness of the sweat that covered Raisa's body and it only added to the desire growing within her.

Hours later when she woke she was alone in bed, again with only the memory of the arms that had held her, the mouth that had teased and tasted her and the hands that had caressed and possessed her.

Chapter Twelve

Raisa walked towards where Nona was sitting. Somehow she knew she would end up here.

Nona sat, as if waiting for her, under the arbor. This had been their place when she was a child. Whenever she needed comforting, Nona had always been there waiting. Somehow she had always known when Raisa needed her.

Raisa walked up to her and sat down quietly at her Nona's feet. Suddenly, the proud dark head came down on the old woman's lap. The old woman caressed the dark locks of hair as she had done so many years ago.

"Cara mia, you have been away so long," Nona said softly.

Raisa closed her eyes. "Yes, Nona."

"Tell me about your friend." The old woman continued to caress the dark head of hair.

Raisa suddenly got up and took a few steps away.

The old woman waited silently.

With her back to the old woman Raisa began to speak.

"I need her," she said simply.

The old woman still waited. Raisa finally turned around and faced her. "I love her." There, she had said it out loud. She locked eyes with Nona defiantly.

"This is the one you have chosen?"

"Yes."

"Good," the old woman said simply.

Raisa's strength seemed to leave her suddenly. And now she looked to the old woman like a frightened child. "You know about me?" She asked softly.

"Cara mia, you are my little girl. I know all about you." She opened her arms as the now sobbing woman went into them. "Te quiero, Cara mia. Te quiero." She held Raisa closer to her as she caressed the dark head of hair and she comforted her child with the reassurance of her love.

****

Late in the afternoon, almost as if by silent understanding, Carolyn walked outside and Raisa was suddenly besides her. She looked different somehow. Both gave each other a shy smile and started walking side by side.

Carolyn looked around her and was amazed with the sheer beauty and an almost dreamy like stillness all around them. Peacocks strolled not too far from them, occasionally opening their feathers like colorful fans, parading them to attract their mates.

"What a beautiful bird," Carolyn commented softly.

"Did you know that the one with the beautiful feathers is the male?"

"Really? Totally unlike humans, huh?"

"Less sure to attract because of its prickly demeanor, perhaps it needs the beautiful feathers," Raisa said seriously staring at the magnificent birds.

Carolyn now looked at her. "I guess they are as blind as some of us."

Raisa looked at her now curiously. "What do you mean?"

"Looking for outer beauty," Carolyn said simply, looking at the birds.

Raisa looked puzzled. "We all look for outer beauty."

"Is that what attracts?" Carolyn asked, still looking at the birds as she started walking again. Raisa started walking next to her.

"Some, it attracts some," Raisa answered uncomfortably.

"Is that how it is with you?" Carolyn stopped now, turning to face her.

Raisa stopped in front of her looking down at her hands as they interlocked nervously.

"Never mind," Carolyn said sadly, walking away.

"Wait!" Raisa caught up with her.

"Is it always this warm this time of the year here?" Carolyn asked in faked politeness.

"You aren't talking to me!" Raisa grabbed her arm and turned her around to face her.

"And who am I talking to?" Carolyn said in exasperation.

Raisa suddenly released her and took a few steps away. She would have normally just walked away and not have bothered; but with Carolyn it was different. It was obvious she was upset as she turned with the wildness in her eyes again but unlike so many other times she had not run.

"Why must you always provoke me?" She asked in exasperation.

"I don't want to fight." Carolyn started walking back to the house.

"What do you want from me?" Raisa demanded in anger.

Carolyn yelled as she kept on walking. "Get a life, you egotistical bitch! And leave me alone."

"I need you!" Raisa yelled back in pain.

Carolyn stopped and turned around slowly. She saw Raisa moving quickly towards her, stopping abruptly in front of her.

"What do you want me to say, Carolyn, that I would want you even if you weren't beautiful?" Raisa asked in agitation.

Carolyn looked down feeling uncomfortable in the situation she found herself in. "No..." she said softly as she looked down.

"I would want you even if I were blind and had never seen you," Raisa said softly. "I can't breathe, eat or sleep without thinking of you."

Carolyn looked up into the eyes that were now soft, filled with uncertainty and fear. "I don't know how to do this." Raisa's words could hardly be heard.

Carolyn raised her hand and caressed the softness of the face in front of her. Her lips were close to Raisa's, but for some reason, unknown to her, still waiting. Then suddenly the words came.

"I love you, Carolyn," Raisa said, barely beyond a whisper and Carolyn's lips met hers tenderly.

Raisa's arms went around her gently, holding her close. When their mouths parted Raisa's eyes avoided the others but her arms still held the woman in them. She was like a deer, caught by a bright light, frozen, and unable to flee.

"I love you, too," Carolyn said softly and Raisa's head came up quickly searching the eyes in front of her.

She stared at Carolyn in disbelief. Suddenly, she pulled her into her arms so tightly that Carolyn could hardly breathe. "Te amo." And this time her mouth was filled with the taste and promise of passion to come.

****

For the next two days they took morning walks and rides together. Then, Raisa would take Simon down to the river to pick sweet fruits and Caroline would set up an afternoon picnic near by.

All that passed between them were warm looks that caressed and spoke of love. The words between them were considerate and tender. They waltzed around one another with care, with the uncertainty and excitement of their newfound love.

Carolyn was touched with the patience that Raisa showed Simon in everything. She was like another woman here at Virago. Nona had been right. Raisa was unique; every moment with her brought new and wonderful surprises. Perhaps it was because she seemed happy. That was the phrase that struck Carolyn as she saw Raisa and Simon running back towards her from the river. Raisa seemed happy.

"I won! I won!" Yelled Simon, full of excitement.

Raisa came up behind him and started tickling him and they both rolled on the ground with abandonment and laughter.

"Come on you two before the ants steal our lunch."

"Okay mom," said Simon as he walked over to his mother.

Raisa lay on the ground looking towards the river as she leaned back on an elbow. Carolyn got up and walked over to her, sitting down, her hand reaching out to caress the dark hair of the woman who had laid siege to her heart.

"Andreas and I used to bathe here when we were children."

"Who is Andreas?"

"My brother. He is away on a buying trip, but he will be here in a few days. He is nothing like me, don't worry," Raisa said with laughter.

"How is he then?"

"He is…he is not like me." Raisa became serious and pensive. Carolyn could see the walls rising.

"Nona would say you are thinking too hard again," Carolyn said. Raisa looked up at her with a smile and then looked back towards the river again.

"Andreas is quiet. There is gentleness about him. Nona says that he is like my mother. But unlike her, he loves this land." She looked all around her. She was quiet for a little while then spoke sadly. "My mother used to love picnics."

"And that makes you sad?" Carolyn asked carefully. This was the first time that they had really spoken of Raisa's family.

"She brought Andreas and I here for a picnic to tell us she was leaving Papa and us. She went back to Italy soon after."

"I'm sorry, sweetheart," Carolyn said lovingly as she caressed her lover's hair. She could feel the pain and anguish that her lover must have felt when being given this news; she could still see it in those eyes. She had come to see in a matter of days that Raisa was not as unfeeling as people thought her to be. And faced with such painful things, who would not shut out loving or needing another human being. To Raisa, it seemed from every word that came from her lips, that love meant pain.

"No need, it was a long time ago," Raisa said, getting up suddenly.

Carolyn reached for her hand and pulled her back down to sit beside her. She held on to her hand as they sat. She could feel the emotions building up inside her.

Raisa looked into her eyes and then looked back out towards the river as she started to speak again. "She hated Venezuela and she ended up hating my father. We were his children so, I guess by association, she hated us." She said nothing after that and Carolyn was shocked into silence by the pain and anger that came out of those words still.

"How old were you?"

"I was seven and Andreas was four when she left," she answered as she played with a patch of grass in front of her.

"Did you ever see her again?"

"No."

"And your father?"

"He died five years ago."

The silence stretched between them. They both were now looking towards the river when Raisa felt Carolyn's hand take hers again and hold it tightly as she said, "I love you, Raisa Andieta."

Chapter Thirteen

They were both coming in from their morning ride when Raisa yelled and her horse took off in a gallop. Carolyn followed.

As they neared the house a man with dark hair came running down the front steps of the hacienda.

Raisa's horse pulled to a stop and went up on its hind legs. Carolyn's breath skipped a beat as she saw Raisa jump off the animal and run into the waiting arms of the man at the steps.

Carolyn slowed down and arrived to hear only some of what was being said. Suddenly, she felt the spark of jealousy come alive.

"God, I've missed you. You are as beautiful as ever," the man said to Raisa as he swung her around in his arms.

"I never stay away from you too long," Raisa said as she ran her hand through the man's hair.

Carolyn's horse bucked, mirroring her own emotions. Raisa turned around and a bright smile appeared on her face. She walked towards Carolyn with an extended hand to help her down the horse.

"Come Cara, there is someone I want you to meet." Raisa pulled Carolyn with her, not noticing the displeasure in her lover's face.

"Andreas, this is Carolyn Stenbeck."

Carolyn looked from Andreas to Raisa and back to Andreas again. Her face now was filled with a great big smile as she put her hand out.

"Welcome to Virago," he said to her with eyes filled with curiosity and admiration.

"Thank you, it's lovely here," Carolyn said honestly.

"I'm glad that you like Virago. Raisa and I grew up here. It's far away from everything but it is best that way sometimes. It's a different world here."

"It's a beautiful world," Carolyn agreed.

Raisa smiled and thought to herself, *She has just won Andreas. How does she do that?*

"I hope you will be able to stay with us a long time."

Raisa suddenly looked at her brother and saw the appreciatory gleam in his eyes. No, no, no, Carolyn was hers; she was going to clear this up right now.

"Well...." Carolyn was interrupted.

"We have no definite plans yet." With that statement Raisa placed her hand possessively around Carolyn's waist.

Carolyn looked at Raisa and smiled indulgently before she continued. "Yes, we have no definite plans yet."

Andreas received the message loud and clear. He could see that there was a lot he had to discuss with his sister. He recognized that she was being possessive of Carolyn and if he didn't know any better, jealous. Yes, they had a lot of talking to do.

They were all suddenly distracted by a boy running excitedly up to them.

"Mom! Mom! Dad is on the phone. He wants to talk to you." The boy was trying to catch his breath and therefore missed Carolyn's eyes as they filled with concern and Raisa's anger began to show.

Andreas however missed nothing.

"Excuse me," Carolyn said as she started walking away.

"Carolyn..." Raisa reached out to try and stop her.

Andreas intervened by holding his sister in place. "Raisa, why don't you introduce this young man to me?"

Carolyn broke eye contact with Raisa and started walking towards the house. Raisa pulled her arms out of Andrea's grasp and stomped away in another direction.

It seems that all is not well, he thought to himself. Then

Andreas directed his attention to the boy in front of him. "Hello," he said extending his hand.

Simon took it and stared at him for a moment. "You are Raisa's brother."

"How did you know?"

"She showed me your photograph."

"Ah…. and you are?"

"Simon Stenbeck."

"Well, then it's nice to meet you. Simon, have you seen the miniature horses yet?"

"What? NO!"

"Come on, let's ask permission. If your mother says yes, I will take you to see them."

****

The conversation with Matt had turned into a shouting match. She was relieved that it had been over when Andreas and Simon came into the room. Carolyn had allowed her son to ride with Andreas to the south pasture to see the miniature horses. Carolyn knew that a confrontation with Raisa was inevitable and she figured the sooner they spoke the better.

She liked Andreas; she could see his gentleness just as Raisa had said. Simon had taken to him right away. After seeing them off Carolyn went in search of Raisa.

****

Carolyn searched for Raisa everywhere. Finally, she went back to the house. She was going upstairs towards her room when she heard loud crashing noises.

When she opened the door she saw chairs upturned and pieces if broken glass all over the floor. She looked towards the vanity and instantly knew what had happened. The smell of perfume permeated the room.

At that moment Raisa walked out of the bathroom. Carolyn looked around in disbelief.

"Why?" Carolyn demanded in anger.

"Because I wanted to!" Raisa yelled back.

"Why?" Carolyn asked again.

"Because it's mine. I can do with it as I please. If I want to smash it into a million pieces then I do it!" Raisa spat out at her.

"Will you do that to me someday?" Carolyn asked suddenly.

All anger left Raisa's face. Suddenly she understood Carolyn's question. And she rushed to her side.

"No," she said softly, trying to reassure her. "No, I would never hurt you."

Carolyn stepped away from her and surveyed the room once more. "Violence seeps into everything in this country, even here."

"You sound like my mother!"

"Perhaps, that is what she ran from!" Carolyn regretted the words as soon as they had come out. Raisa bolted and ran out like an injured animal.

"Wait! Raisa, wait!"

****

Carolyn got to the verandah only to see Raisa gallop away. She would have to wait until she came back to talk to her. She kept telling herself she should never have said that. Raisa had trusted her with her pain and she had used it against her to hurt her. Carolyn had done the same thing that everyone else had. She had hurt her.

"Oh Raisa, I'm so sorry," Carolyn said sadly as she walked back inside.

Nona met her as she walked into the house.

"She will come back."

"I hurt her," Carolyn said as tears filled her eyes.

"She is wild inside. Very much like her father," Nona said softly. "Adele loved him but in the end..." Nona could not finish. Her head bent down in sadness.

"Nona, what happened with her mother? She told me some things... but I don't think she herself understands what happened."

Nona looked at her with doubt. "I can't..."

"Please help me. I love Raisa. Whatever is chasing her is coming between us."

"Come." Nona walked to the verandah, sitting down in a wicker chair. Carolyn sat in another opposite her.

"Adele, Raisa's mother, married Martin, her father, when she was barely 19. I worked for her family in Italy then. Adele was beautiful and vibrant. She was very much like Raisa in some ways. But of course not quite." Nona smiled indulgently. "Martin was handsome and charming. They fell passionately in love. Adele's father objected to the marriage and they eloped. Adele got in touch with her family about two years later. They loved her so some ties were repaired,"

Nona now took a deep breath before she started again. "She was lonely for her homeland and her people. That's where I come in. I agreed to come and help her with Raisa. She was expecting another child then, Andreas. Right away I noticed that things were not going well between them. Adele was short tempered and Martin was not indulging."

Carolyn waited patiently.

"After Andreas was born, things just seemed to get worse as time went by. Martin showed favoritism to his son. He was the male child Martin had wanted and Adele fought with him constantly because he ignored Raisa. Still, there was this thing between them that kept the marriage going... until it all exploded one night." Nona became very sad and quite suddenly seemed to age.

"They fought, and I think that things just went too far. Martin had been drinking. Adele ran out of the house and he went after her. When she returned her clothes were torn and dirty. Worst of all, she did not speak for days. When Martin came back in the morning he locked himself up in his study and drank for days. She told me she was leaving him. She said she had to leave or this land would kill her. She said she would make arrangements later for the children and me. She never did; Raisa never forgave her. I can still see my little girl... she stood on this verandah everyday for a month, waiting. She never believed that her mother would really leave her,

75

you see."

Nona looked up at Carolyn now. She could see the questions and the horror on her face.

"I never heard from Adele again. Martin never spoke of her and refused to have anyone speak her name. He never allowed the children to go out of the country even when Adele's parents requested to see them."

"Oh Nona, how awful. Raisa was just a child."

"I don't think she ever forgave either Adele or Martin. But, at least in her mind, Martin stayed. She became the son he wanted."

"And Raisa, the little girl, just got lost along the way," Carolyn said sadly.

"She is still there when she puts her head on my lap. When she is tender and out there in the land that she loves, then she is my little girl again. She was adventurous as a child. A little too wild but she was kind and tender. She adored her mother. When she finally accepted that Adele was not coming back for her, a part of her just died inside, I think."

"No wonder she is so angry," Carolyn whispered out loud.

"She is fighting herself all the time. Sometimes, it is stronger than she is," Nona said sadly. "You also hate this land, don't you? Like Adele did?"

Carolyn looked at the old woman and nodded. "She has been so different here until today. I fear the violence Nona. I fear Raisa sometimes, too." Carolyn lowered her head.

Nona put her hand over the younger woman's. "She is like that horse she loves to ride. His name is Furioso. Furioso, is wild and head strong, hard to handle and won't let anyone ride him, except for Raisa. That animal is a beast except with her. He loves her and she loves him. He would never throw her and she would never whip him. Do you understand, Carolyn?"

"I think I understand, Nona. I just don't know if I can live with it."

"You have to look beyond what you see and see what you love."

Carolyn looked at the old woman and did not understand somehow.

"Adele loved Martin. But, they stopped looking and all that was left was fear and anger."

Carolyn looked up as Raisa was riding up to the house. Carolyn got up and kissed Nona on the cheek.

"Thank you. I understand a little better now."

"Go, Cara mia. Go to her," Nona said gently and walked back inside the house.

Carolyn waited as Raisa got off the horse and someone walked over to take Furioso from her. But before she handed the reins over she caressed the horse's mane and spoke gently as she rubbed her face against the animal's head.

Raisa walked up to the verandah and passed Carolyn without a word. Carolyn took a deep breath and followed her.

****

Raisa walked into her bedroom and started taking clothes off as she walked into the bathroom. Carolyn came in and locked the door behind her. She could hear the shower going.

"Well, it's now or never," Carolyn murmured, taking off her own clothes.

****

Raisa was a storm of emotions, as they all whirled around inside her. She was angry, hurt, and she felt caged and full of raging energy.

She didn't hear the shower door open. When she felt arms come around her she turned in anger, ready to strike. Instantly, she saw Carolyn cringe. Raisa reached for her and pulled her to her desperately.

Carolyn melted into the arms that held her. Her hands started stroking Raisa's back and slowly she felt the woman in her arms start to relax. When Raisa put her head down on her shoulder Carolyn said the only thing she could and she knew it wouldn't be enough to express her regret. "I'm sorry."

Raisa's arms tightened around her.

"Please forgive me. I'm so very sorry," Carolyn whispered into Raisa's hair. Raisa nodded and Carolyn kept reassuring her with caresses and phrases of love.

Chapter Fourteen

Raisa sat at the head of the dinner table with Carolyn on her right and Simon on her left. Andreas sat on the other end. Dinner had been pleasant and cordial.

"So when does the procession start tomorrow?" Andreas asked as he was eating his dessert.

Raisa looked up at Carolyn. Andreas was oblivious.

"This flan is really good. Nona really outdid herself," Andreas said looking down at his dessert.

"What procession?" Asked Carolyn nervously.

"I forgot about the invitations to the Copeco executives completely," Raisa said as she placed her hand over Carolyn's.

Andreas looked up and realized that there was going to be a problem. He just listened as the women continued to speak. Carolyn looked visibly upset. Simon looked up suddenly realizing his mother sounded odd.

"How could you forget?" Carolyn said as she got up to leave the room. She turned to Andreas. "Please excuse me, Andreas, I'm tired, it's been a long day. Simon darling, finish your lovely dessert and come to my room when you are done."

"Okay, mommy."

Carolyn left the dinning room. Raisa sat, looking into space, visibly distraught to anyone who knew her.

"Raisa, is my father coming tomorrow?" Simon asked innocently.

Raisa turned towards the child, almost as if it suddenly hit her. She looked at Andreas and he quickly understood the problem.

"Raisa?" Simon put his small hand on her arm.

Raisa turned towards the child again. Her face relaxed as she looked at the child that to her so much resembled his mother. She reached out, caressed his hair and smiled, expressing the softness of her emotions. "You are so much like your mother, Simon."

Simon smiled back at her. "Yeah, my dad says that all the time, too."

Raisa smiled sadly at the boy and looked down at her plate again. "Yes, Simon, your father will probably be coming tomorrow." She spoke barely above a whisper. Then she raised her eyes and met Andrea's gaze.

"Good, I miss my dad," Simon said as he was finishing his dessert.

Raisa just stared at the boy.

"Well, Simon why don't you and I play a game of chess before you go up to your mother?" Andreas asked looking at Raisa. She looked towards her brother and understood instantly that he was giving her time to talk to Carolyn.

"Sure, that would be great, Andreas."

"Yes, thank you, Andreas," Raisa said to her brother. "Simon, you enjoy your game with Andreas; I'm going to speak to your mother and tell her that you will be up after your game."

Simon smiled at her and nodded. Raisa got up and went to find Carolyn.

****

Raisa walked in and immediately noticed Carolyn sitting in front of the vanity staring into the glass. She had not even heard Raisa come in.

"Carolyn…"

"Why?"

"I forgot. I swear." Raisa knelt down in front of her.

"I can't face Matt tomorrow. I can't do this with Simon here. I need time." Carolyn got more agitated by the second.

"Nothing will happen, Carolyn. No one is taking you from me," Raisa said with conviction.

"Don't you see that this has the makings of a disaster?" Carolyn said in exasperation as she got up and walked away from Raisa. "I don't want Simon dragged into this!"

"I would never hurt Simon!" Raisa lashed out.

Carolyn turned to her now. "With Matt here anything can happen! Surely you don't think he won't come?" Carolyn argued back in frustration.

"Nothing will happen, I promise you. Simon will be all right." Raisa tried to sound convincing but even she knew that things might very well get totally out of hand.

Carolyn ran to her and hid her face in Raisa's neck. "I can't lose my son, Raisa, I can't lose my son." Raisa held her tightly.

"Nothing will take either of you from me, Cara mia. Nothing," Raisa whispered into Carolyn's hair.

****

The next morning the Copeco executives started arriving along with their families. Both Raisa and Andreas greeted them. Accommodations were prepared in another section of the house. Towards the end of lunch, most were relaxing around the pool, children ran about and joyous voices filled the air. Carolyn was talking to a few women of the Copeco wives she had known from other such meetings at the club.

Raisa's eyes would intermittently search for her to reassure herself that Carolyn was still there and still hers.

Around two in the afternoon a land rover pulled up in front of the hacienda and out stepped Matt Stenbeck. Almost by radar, Simon spotted him.

"Daddy!" Simon sprinted towards his father as two sets of

eyes followed him, one set with fear, the other with rage.

****

Raisa watched Matt pick up his son and hug him. She noticed when his eyes searched and found Carolyn. And, as she saw him start towards her, she started walking as well only to be stopped by Andreas.

"Let go of me!" She growled behind her teeth.

"Calm down, you don't want to do this. Not now. Think Raisa, think!" Andreas held her by her arm.

"She's mine!" Her eyes turned to him in anger and in fear. It was the first time that Andreas saw the vulnerability in her.

"Yes, she loves you. No need to storm the barracks. Play to win. You won't win this way. All you will do is make a scene and you will involve Carolyn in a scandal. Is that what you want? Do you want Simon to see it too?" Andreas immediately knew he had reached her. For now, Raisa was rational.

"I won't lose her. I can't," she finished softly.

"And you won't," Andreas said kindly to his sister. He had never seen Raisa like this. She had always been the strong one. The one who fought their father so that he could stay in Virago and lead the life he loved. She was the one who kept Copeco going and just naturally took charge. He had always looked on her as not needing what most held dear. And now, he was touched by her vulnerability. For the first time he felt he had to protect her. Andreas followed her eyes and watched as Matt approached Carolyn with Simon by the hand.

****

"Mr. Stenbeck, hello. I am Andreas Andieta," Andreas said as he extended his hand in welcome.

"Hello, Mr. Andieta. Virago is extraordinary," Matt answered as he shook Andreas's hand.

"Thank you. It has been in my family for five generations," Andreas said proudly.

"I was telling my wife that my flight was delayed, that's why I arrived late."

"Well, the important thing is that you are here," Andreas said politely. "We have had the pleasure of having Carolyn and Simon here with us for a few days."

"Yes," Matt said as he looked towards Carolyn. She looked away.

Before Matt could say anything else, Andreas intervened. "Why don't you get yourself a drink at the bar by the pool. That will take the tiredness away. Here in the jungle we take things a little slower but it's worth it."

"It is far away from everything," Matt said diplomatically.

"Dad, Andreas and Raisa have miniature horses here," Simon interrupted excitedly. Matt noticed as Andreas tousled the boy's hair affectionately and bestowed him with a smile.

"I'm glad that you have enjoyed the visit, Simon," Andreas said indulgently.

Carolyn caught Andreas's eye, then looked away. Andreas did not have to guess what Carolyn was looking at. He turned just in time to see Raisa within feet of them. He just prayed that she would keep it together.

"Andreas, the men are ready for the hunt. They're waiting on you. Will you be joining them, Matt?" Raisa asked Matt.

Matt was about to answer no when Andreas interceded.

"You can't miss this, Mr. Stenbeck. The boars are huge. Of course he will come. All of us men are going." Andreas gave him no way of refusing politely.

"Yes, of course I'll come. Please, call me Matt."

"Then it's settled. Matt, Antonio will take you to your room so that you can change into something more appropriate and then we will all be on our way." Andreas motioned a young man over to them to attend to their new guest.

"Come along darling, we can catch up while I change," Matt said as he took Carolyn by the arm. Raisa was about to follow but Andreas stopped her.

"Simon, you stay here while I talk to mom." Matt looked back and stopped his son from following.

Andreas noticed the disappointment in the boy. "Simon, the boys over there are starting a volleyball game. Hurry and you can play with them."

Simon looked at the direction he was pointing, smiled and ran toward the children.

Raisa couldn't stand it and tried pulling away. "Let me go! You don't understand!"

"I do understand. She has to sever the ties herself, Raisa. You can't do that for her," Andreas insisted.

"You don't understand!"

"Yes, I do," Andreas said in a soft voice.

"You can't possibly. Andreas, I need her!" Raisa said in desperation to her brother.

"You think because I don't act like you that I can't feel as strongly as you?"

Raisa looked deep into her brother's eyes.

"I understand, Raisa. I understand."

"Andreas..." she began to say gently.

"Another day, not today. Only one passionate love affair per Andieta at a time."

He smiled at her. "Come, let's see to our guests." He led his sister back to the others.

****

"What's going on Carolyn? What the fuck is going on here?" Matt demanded.

"Stop yelling!"

"I want this insanity to stop. We will be civil for the next few days and then leave," Matt said as he started unpacking.

"I'm not going back," Carolyn said softly.

"Of course you are. You can't get proper medical treatment here. The doctor said you might be over emotional because of the baby." He continued to unpack.

"What? What are you talking about?" Carolyn looked confused.

"The doctor called and I spoke with him. Why didn't you tell me?" Matt now looked up to meet her eyes.

"It can't be true," she said weakly.

"You didn't know, did you?" Matt asked her in confusion.

"No," Carolyn said and found a place to sit before her legs gave out.

"Well, that explains your odd behavior. Apparently the doctor says some women get incredibly sensitive and overemotional. So you see, it's quite natural. It will all go back to normal when your hormones settle. It's time Simon had a brother or sister anyway," Matt said half to himself while dressing.

Carolyn sat in shocked silence.

"What I don't understand is how you came to be here. I didn't realize you knew Raisa Andieta so well. I just thought your attending those luncheons was a waste of time. But now, well, to know her so well can only work in our favor."

"Matt, please be quiet," Carolyn finally said as she pressed her temples with her hands.

Matt turned and was about to say something when he noticed how pale she had suddenly gotten.

"Are you feeling ill, Carolyn?"

"What do you think?" She got up, agitation plainly showing on her face.

"You will feel better…"

"No! I won't feel better! I don't believe you. You're lying!"

"Call your doctor if you don't believe me," Matt said in restrained anger.

"Oh God, no," she whimpered as she sat back down again. Her whole world was running through her fingers. How would she tell Raisa? This question kept going through her mind.

"Carolyn, I know that things have not been perfect between us..."

At that statement something inside her snapped. "What did you say? Were you actually going to say that perhaps something could possibly be going wrong between us?" Carolyn yelled in mockery.

"Carolyn, you are over reacting."

"You son of a bitch!" She went at him and he grabbed her hands, pushing her onto the bed.

"Calm down. Don't embarrass me, Carolyn!"

"I will never go back with you. Never!" She yelled from where she lay.

"Yes, you will," Matt said as he walked over to a chair, sat down, and started putting his boots on. "You won't leave without Simon. And that child growing inside you is mine too. This country recognizes my right over them, Carolyn!"

"How could I have married a monster like you?"

Matt did not bother to answer.

"Matt, it's over. Let me go. Please, I beg you."

"No," he muttered under his breath.

"I don't love you, Matt," she said barely above a whisper.

"Fine."

"Matt, let me go. You know how this baby was created. Let me go before all the good is gone."

"This child was created with passion, Carolyn!"

"You raped me! That's not passion!" She could no longer hold back the sobbing.

"You are my wife. I have the right," he said, unable to look at her. "All right Carolyn, you can have your divorce. But Simon stays with me."

"You know I won't leave my son, you know that!"

"Then be the wife I know you can be and let go of this mad idea." He demanded. "Think about what I've said, Carolyn."

On that note, he strode out of the room leaving her to deal with her torment.

****

Carolyn stood by the window and watched as the hunting party rode away. For a moment she saw Raisa look towards her. Raisa, being the CEO of Copeco, rode with the men. She was the only woman who rode off but not before looking back and seeing Carolyn looking at her from the window. Then Raisa turned and galloped away.

Carolyn's hand was shaking as it went to her temple again. *This can't be true,* she told herself over and over again. *This can't be true.*

She had wanted desperately to leave Matt for a long time now. But she couldn't take Simon out of the country without his permission. One night her no's had not worked and ... she closed her eyes as the tears ran down her face. Then the whole thing with Raisa started. She couldn't think straight after that. Her emotions ran from hot to cold. She had accepted her desire for Raisa but she was overwhelmed with her need to flee from Matt. That afternoon when she called Raisa for help she was desperate. Matt had told her in no uncertain terms that he would take her whether she wanted it or not. Carolyn's only thought was to run. And run she did; into Raisa Andieta's arms.

Raisa loved her, she knew that. But her lover had so much baggage to deal with of her own. She had to make Raisa understand. Raisa would help her. She had to.

Her hands went protectively across her abdomen. She would have to tell her the truth. There was no other way. She had to trust that Raisa would love her enough.

.

Chapter Fifteen

Finally, the riders returned with two boars as their trophies. There was a planned dinner that evening so everyone went to their bedrooms to clean up and change for the festivities.

Raisa did not get to see Carolyn until that evening. When Raisa entered the room only a few of her executives and their wives had come down. Raisa instantly saw Carolyn speaking to Maria Cabaler and started walking towards her.

"Good evening," Raisa said. Carolyn had not seen her enter the room and turned around to look into the eyes that made her heart soar each and every time.

Both Maria and Carolyn responded, "Good evening."

"Maria, will you please give me a minute with Mrs. Stenbeck?" Raisa asked graciously

"Of course," the other woman said as she walked away.

Raisa then turned and smiled at Carolyn. "I missed you today," she said barely above a whisper.

Carolyn returned the smile. "I missed you too, sweetheart."

"Have I told you how much I like it when you call me sweetheart?" Raisa felt the joy grow inside her. Carolyn was looking at her with eyes filled with love. She would not leave her. And knowing that made her feel giddy with happiness.

"Does it?"

"Yes, it does, Cara mia."

"Then I shall have to call you that more often, won't I?"

Carolyn said lovingly.

This was the perfect time, Raisa told herself. She took a deep breath. "Carolyn, I want to spend the rest…"

Mario Carabel, Maria's husband, interrupted her. "Good evening, Ms. Andieta, Mrs. Stenbeck," he said with a smile. "Have you seen my wife?" He asked pleasantly.

"Good evening, Mario. I saw your wife going out to the verandah," Raisa said politely.

"Thank you." As he was about to leave he turned towards Carolyn. "Oh, and by the way Mrs. Stenbeck, congratulations on the new baby. Matt seems very happy."

Triumphantly, Matt appeared and put his arm around Carolyn's waist. "I'm sorry dear but I was so excited with the news I had to tell Mario."

Carolyn stared at Raisa who immediately shut her out. "Are you expecting a baby, Carolyn?" To her credit, Raisa asked before judging her, Carolyn told herself.

Carolyn could not deny it. "Yes."

Raisa smiled and the coldness from her eyes made Carolyn shiver. "Congratulations Matt, please excuse me." Raisa walked away from all of them and left the room.

****

Without their hostess the party broke up early. Matt had taken Simon for a walk and Carolyn waited for Raisa. Nona had told her she had gone out on Furioso. Carolyn still hoped that they could work it all out.

She was looking out of a window towards the fields as Raisa came into the room wearing her riding attire.

Carolyn turned around to face her and said with all the tenderness she could express. "I love you."

"You love me?" Raisa said mockingly. "When were you going to tell me? You are worse than a whore! At least they are honest." Raisa kept her distance.

"Don't, please don't." Carolyn could barely speak. The day was taking its toll and she was barely hanging on.

"Well, you made a first class fool out of me."

"Raisa, let me explain." Carolyn walked towards her.

"Are you pregnant, Carolyn?" She demanded.

"Yes, but…"

"No but's. I am so full of rage that I want to just scream!" Raisa spat at her.

"Let me talk to you!' Carolyn demanded.

"Don't you dare raise your voice to me!" Raisa lunged at her, grabbing her by the face as she pushed her against the wall. "I honored you. I didn't treat you like the whore that you are. I loved you. I laid my world at your feet and all along you were with him. You lied to me. You said you were only mine. All the while I was inside you, all the times my mouth tasted you. All those times… Oh God!" Raisa released her and put some distance between them again. The rage inside her was pouring out.

"Go before I kill you," Raisa said softly with her back to Carolyn. And somehow the softness of her voice was more menacing then the screaming.

Raisa felt Carolyn's arms come from behind her and she pulled away quickly, facing her now.

"Don't come near me! If you do I know that I will hit you," Raisa growled. Carolyn kept walking towards her as Raisa walked backwards until she was against a wall.

Carolyn's eyes were pleading as she continued her approach. She leaned against Raisa's body as she remembered the words that Nona had spoken. And she somehow knew that Raisa would not hurt her.

Carolyn leaned deeper into Raisa and her head leaned on her shoulder, her eyes closed and she began to cry.

Raisa's head was leaning back against the wall, her eyes closed. She could feel Carolyn's body against her and she knew that she was crying. She could not control what she did next. Her arms came up behind Carolyn's back as she held her.

"I didn't know I was pregnant until today," Carolyn said between tears. "All that I said to you was true." She was suddenly pulled away from the warmth of Raisa's body.

"For God's sake, don't lie!" Raisa walked away from her again. She walked like a person beaten by exhaustion. She ran her fingers through her hair, then sat down on a sofa close by, her head falling back. "Don't lie anymore, Carolyn. I can't…"

"Raisa, when I called you that day I was desperate. I had had a fight with Matt that day. We had not been living as man and wife for a long time."

Raisa's head lifted from the sofa and she was now listening.

Carolyn became visibly nervous. "I wanted a divorce but he wouldn't let me take Simon out of Venezuela. I couldn't leave without Simon." Carolyn looked away but continued. Raisa was looking at her intently. "One night, Matt got home and … I…" she could not continue.

"You fucked him," Raisa said coldly.

Carolyn faced her with a face full of pain. "He raped me." She began to cry, covering face with her hands.

Raisa stared in disbelief. She got up not knowing whether or not to believe what she had heard.

"Please understand. Please, I love you," Carolyn began to beg her.

Raisa grabbed her by the arms and stared into her eyes. "You aren't lying," Raisa said as a whole new rage took over. Nothing would stop the storm now.

Carolyn felt as if she had been physically struck by the coldness emanating from Raisa. Raisa released her and walked over the mantle of the great room. She removed the rifle and walked over to the cabinet. She struck the glass with the rifle butt and grabbed a box of bullets. Carolyn stared in horror.

"No, no, you can't." Carolyn rushed over to Raisa as she loaded and cocked the weapon, but Raisa neither saw nor heard her.

Andreas walked in from one door as Matt was walking in by another. It all happened at once. Raisa and Carolyn's world exploded around them within seconds.

Carolyn tried to pull her back, but Raisa's arm struck back, knocking her to the floor as Simon entered the room. Simon saw his mother fall, blood coming from her mouth.

Raisa pointed the gun at Matt as Andreas rushed her. The shot went off into the air. Matt came towards her, and as she succeeded in pushing Andreas away she hit Matt with the butt of the rifle in the gut and he fell on his knees gasping for air. She screamed in rage and butted him in the head. Blood went everywhere as Matt fell to the floor.

Andreas and Carolyn stared in horror as she cocked the gun again to shoot Matt before Simon covered his father with his body. Raisa had the rifle pointed at his chest.

"Get away from my father!" Simon yelled at the top of his lungs.

The hatred in the boy's eyes stunned her. Andreas came up from behind her and took the rifle out of her hands, pulling her back with him.

"I hate you! I hate you! You hurt my father. Mommy! Mommy!" Simon cried.

Raisa looked around in confusion and noticed Carolyn on the floor as blood ran down her nose and mouth.

Raisa was in a haze. She looked around her and all the horror rushed in at once and her world collapsed in front of her as she leaned against her brother in silence.

Carolyn went to Simon who sobbed in her arms. "She hurt you too, Mommy. I want to go. She killed my Daddy, she killed my Daddy!"

Matt stirred and started moving as blood ran down the side of his head. "Dad!" Simon left his mother's arms and went to his father. Matt sat up slowly.

Carolyn looked at Raisa in desolation. Their eyes locked for a brief moment. Carolyn broke the connection. The whole world reeled around them. It was over.

S. Anne Gardner

Chapter Sixteen

Suddenly, all the sounds of the horror around her filled her head. Some servants rushed in followed by Nona. Simon was sobbing. Carolyn seemed frozen and Andreas held on to Raisa from behind. Raisa seemed like a rag doll slumped against him, lifeless.

Nona directed the servants to lock all the doors and windows of the room and keep all of the other guests out. The shots had awakened many of the people in the house and the buzzing of voices could be heard getting closer.

Andreas snapped out of it first. He turned Raisa around and sat her down in a nearby chair. She did not move. He believed her to be in shock, but when he released her she got up quickly and tried grabbing for Carolyn,

"Carolyn! Carolyn!" Raisa screamed as Andreas pulled her back.

Simon's cries became more hysterical as he reached for his mother. "Mommy! Mommy!"

"Carolyn! Please.... Please, Carolyn!" Raisa continued to beg.

Matt started getting up. Nona directed one of the servants to help him to the sofa as she went to Raisa.

"Mi angel, ella no es para ti," Nona gently told Raisa that Carolyn was not for her.

"Yo la amo. Ella es mia, Nona. Yo la amo!" Raisa was screaming, insisting that she loved Carolyn, and that she belonged to her.

"No, mi angel, ella no es para ti." Nona held her tightly.

Raisa released a scream that let out all the pain her soul held inside and sobbed in Nona's arms. "Yo la amo....Yo la amo," she whimpered as a child. As she fell to the ground, Nona knelt down, took her in her arms again and rocked her in her embrace.

Andreas went to Carolyn and helped her up. Their eyes met briefly. "I think you can still fix this," he whispered to her.

"No...we can't." Carolyn held Simon to her and walked over to Matt.

****

Andreas took over. To Raisa the world seemed to stop. She knew that it was over. She had seen it in Carolyn's eyes. And yet somehow she could not accept it.

Raisa woke from a daze and realized that she had lost track of time. She knew that a doctor had been called and that Matt would recover from his concussion. She had not killed him. He had taken from her all that mattered to her and she hated him now more than ever. Then she realized that Carolyn would be gone with him. Like when her mother had left...she could no longer really hear or smell or taste. And somehow she knew that she had to find Carolyn. She had to find Carolyn now!

She walked out of her room with a purpose. All she knew was that she had to find Carolyn. She had to make her stay. She would not let her go. She had to make her....

Raisa shook her head. She felt out of control. All she knew for certain was that her life was ending. Nothing had prepared her for this. She was complete emotion, unbridled and unrestrained.

She searched the house and then ran to the verandah that wrapped itself around the second floor of the hacienda. As she turned her head she saw the silhouette of Carolyn. Instinctively,

Carolyn turned her head at that same moment. Both eyes locked; one set unsure the other filled with sadness.

Raisa stood in front of Carolyn before she had a chance to catch her breath. Raisa reached out for her and Carolyn took a step back.

"No," she mouthed.

Raisa stood rooted to the spot, as her hands reached out for her, a soft cry of pain escaped her lips. "Don't go…"

Carolyn just shook her head as the tears ran down her face. "I can't stay here…try to understand," she sobbed. Carolyn covered her mouth to control her sobbing.

Raisa went to her and took her in her arms roughly. She tried taking Carolyn's mouth with her own, but Carolyn shoved her away.

"No!" Carolyn put distance between them. "No! Wanting isn't enough! I can't stay here! Everywhere I look… all around me…this violence never ends." Carolyn wrapped her arms around her stomach. "I won't bring another child into this country…. I can't live like this…." she sobbed.

"We can leave Venezuela together. I'll go wherever you want," Raisa begged. Her eyes were wild. Carolyn could see the desperation there

"No…I can't do this," Carolyn said softly, looking down.

"You can't, or you won't!"

Raisa did not try to touch her again. After several minutes Carolyn looked up and, as she did, was surprised by the woman who stood before her.

The Raisa who stood in front of her now was cool and in control. She took a step towards the verandah railing and then slowly turned around.

"Copeco has offices in Texas. Matt will do well there. He will get a cushy job that he will accept. Your son will live in a civilized country and your child will be an American. You will become one of the many other Copeco wives. Your husband will have a mistress or an affair occasionally and then will go home and fuck you when he has time."

Carolyn stood speechless, in shock at the delivery of this speech. "Raisa…" she began to say.

Raisa raised her hand to silence her. "No need to thank me.

One day you will curse me, because this is your punishment, Carolyn. You are going to curse me for this."

Carolyn took a step back as the woman in front of her became a stranger.

"Your blood will burn as mine does. You will dream of my touch and of my mouth. You will want me everyday of your life. I curse you, Carolyn! I will never touch you again!" Raisa turned around and walked away.

Within a few days, Andreas had arranged it all. Matt, Carolyn and Simon were flown back to Caracas. Matt had accepted the apology and understood the conditions without saying a word. He accepted his new promotion and they were all planning their move back to the US within the next few weeks. Carolyn never saw Raisa again before leaving Hacienda Virago. Matt never requested an explanation.

Chapter Seventeen

Carolyn notified the school that Simon would not be returning. She contacted her parents who were delighted at the news of their return to the US. In two weeks, she would be leaving Venezuela.

The city seemed tenser since the last time she had been there. More political graffiti seemed to be everywhere. Public transportation went on strike. People took to the street and the army was called out to restore order.

It all happened quickly. Troops took over the radio stations and La Casa Rosada. Like a powder keg, the fire had burned out the fuse and it exploded. Civil war erupted. Militia took to the streets. Shots were seen, like fireworks, from a distance. Helicopters flew overhead. For hours one could hear tanks and machine guns being fired. The world of fear that Carolyn had foreseen had come to pass. Looting started and the populace took to the streets.

One night, Matt had gone out and did not come back. The servants left, attempting to get home to their loved ones and Carolyn was left with Simon alone. When she heard a few helicopters fly overhead, followed soon after by banging on her door, she thought her knees would give out. Simon hid his face in fear. Carolyn knew that houses were being looted.

Suddenly, she heard the shattering of wood and she watched as three men entered the house. Carolyn held Simon to her tightly. Then she saw Raisa.

99

"Come on," she called to her. "You can't stay here…now!"

Carolyn followed her out of the house and into the helicopter that was now a few yards away from the house. The shots could be heard even past the noise of the propellers. Raisa put her hand out to her and Carolyn took it. She got in as Simon was hoisted up and strapped in by one of the men who had entered the house.

It was all so unreal. Raisa reached over and strapped her in, signaled the pilot, and the helicopter took to the air. Carolyn looked down in time to see men running into the grounds and shooting at them as they flew higher and higher. A bullet came close and she felt Raisa's arms around her.

Within minutes they were landing. She looked up in a daze and realized that they were in Maiquetia Airport, just outside Caracas. Suddenly, she was being hoisted out of the helicopter again. She could see Simon being carried towards a waiting jet.

Carolyn turned around and felt Raisa's mouth on hers instantly. Raisa suddenly released her and said loud enough in her ear as she held her to her. "Now I don't owe you a thing. Next time I see you, stay away from me or I'll kill you."

Raisa pushed her away from her and Carolyn was pulled towards the waiting airplane. Shock and hurt still showed in her face. She went up the stairs of the airplane clumsily and she could see Matt and Simon together inside. Carolyn turned around and looked towards Raisa once more before the door was closed.

Raisa stood as her hair swirled wildly. She saw when Carolyn turned around and she stood there as the door closed. She was still in the same place minutes after the plane had already gone.

Someone tugged her arm and she saw them signaling towards the car. She went into the waiting automobile and picked up the phone.

"Ms. Andieta, we have him," she heard from the other side of the connection.

"Good, I'll meet you at the country club. Is the TV station still under our control?"

"Yes, V-Vision is under our control."

"Good, I'll be there soon."

Raisa signaled the driver and the bulletproof automobile took off at great speed followed by four other vehicles. Raisa put on the sunglasses that she was well known for wearing. In a few hours she would either be on her way to unimaginable power or to certain death. She had made sure she had kept her word. That's what she told herself. She had gotten Carolyn out. Carolyn was safe, she had seen to that. Now she only had one thing to focus on. She was playing to win or to die. And at this moment she didn't much care which.

Chapter Eighteen

That the military coup in Venezuela had failed was reported by all news agencies. At the last minute, the president had been flown out by helicopter. Said helicopter had landed at the Country Club close to Las Colinas Residences and then the President had somehow managed to get to the V-Vision television station. He had barricaded himself in the television station with loyal troops surrounding it.

The president had appealed to the people. Support from the military that he did not seem to have previously, quickly appeared; within a few weeks the city was, once again, under his control. The military had brought back order and those responsible had been captured. Soon after, it became quite obvious that the balance of power had changed. It became apparent to those that understood how things really worked that Copeco was now the major player.

Within a few months things began to stabilize. Elections came and went but that was expected. Within a few years, Raisa's control over almost everything that moved, transpired, lived and breathed was absolute. Her power was all-encompassing. Copeco was the most powerful conglomerate that Latin America had ever known. Copeco and its subsidiaries grew and multiplied.

Chapter Nineteen

A woman screamed in the night. All knew better than to try and assist. The servants had learned to not hear or see anything. They were well paid for their silence. Women came and went. All left better or worse for wear, but none complained. Their hands were always full of money, and if truth were told, given the chance they would keep coming back for more.

It was dark and the two figures on the bed were finally still. Raisa got up and walked naked to the French doors. She flung them open and let the wind rush in. A storm was coming. One could smell the earth and the charge in the air. It was a big storm.

Raisa walked out on the verandah and let the wind caress her body. The moonlight caressed her body as her face looked up and she allowed herself to feel its touch. All she could hear was the wind swirling around her. She fed off the storm. Raisa drew deep within herself and suddenly she could hear music playing. Lighting flashed and thunder could be heard crashing loudly against the earth. She was once again surrounded in darkness.

Out of the corner of her eye she saw a shadow. She turned and stared, not believing, and yet yearning to touch. She heard the thunder once more. All the elements were playing tricks on her. The shadow reached out for her.

"Carolyn!" Raisa took the woman into her arms and her mouth sought lips that burned with passion and promise.

The body in her arms did not fit. The mouth that she kissed was not as warm and did not beckon. She shut her eyes tightly and pushed the body she held away. The lighting illuminated the balcony and Raisa could see the girl on the floor. As usual, they all looked at her with fear in the end.

"Go back inside!" Raisa shouted. The girl got up and went back into the bedroom. Raisa looked around and felt foolish, anger filling her once more.

She entered the room with all her demons once more inside her. The young woman was getting dressed. "I thought you might want to be alone," the young woman said softly.

The lightning flashed outside once more, soon after followed by the roaring thunder "Not yet. I still want to fuck. Walk over there and bend over". Raisa walked up to her, grabbed the dress and ripped it as the thunder rang out even louder than before.

****

Carolyn sat up in bed with a start. She looked around, not knowing exactly what she expected. She looked towards the flashing lights visible from the windows. A storm was brewing. That's what must have woken her, she tried to rationalize. She looked next to her and saw that Matt was sleeping soundly. She lay back down slowly and stared into the darkness.

She hated waking up in the middle of the night like this. Carolyn always felt as if the darkness mocked her. The darkness that once upon a time had been cool and welcoming now felt foreign and menacing.

She got up and went out of her bedroom, as she always did when waking in the middle of the night, which was often in the past years. Carolyn walked through the house in the dark, first checking on Simon and then on her daughter Amanda. Confirming that both her children were safe and asleep she went to the great room of the house and sat on the lavishly plush white sofa. She seemed to sink into its softness. Her arms went protectively around her body.

Quite suddenly she was filled with a need that she had felt so many times before. Carolyn closed her eyes and allowed her head to fall back. It hurt so much to remember and yet she was cursed not to be able to forget.

She had cursed her, Raisa had. Carolyn could still remember the words and the look in Raisa's eyes. She had cursed her to want what she could not have. Carolyn looked around her; opulence and wealth surrounded her. Matt needed to show off his success at every moment. This huge house was just one more showpiece for him, like his wife and his children.

Her children were healthy and seemed happy, she told herself over and over again. Most women would love to be her. Matt was doing well in the company. His ace always being that the head of Copeco herself favored him. He was admired by his colleges and had gone far within the corporate ladder. He was one of Copeco's golden boys.

Carolyn had never seen Raisa after she had left Venezuela almost 10 years ago. Raisa had kept her word. All that she had promised Carolyn had come to pass. Raisa had not tried to contact her or so much as interfere in her life. Carolyn had not heard her voice or even seen a photograph of her and yet Raisa was more a part of her than she was when they had been lovers. Raisa was under her skin and in her blood. Raisa filled her mind and her dreams.

Again, in desperation, Carolyn looked around the room. A heavy wind blew the French doors open and that same wind filled the space around her. The sounds of the storm and its passion swirled around her and Carolyn cried out in pain into the maelstrom. She closed her eyes only to feel the hunger that would never be quenched. She was filled with a need to touch and feel and taste and want and want and want, without end. "Raisa..." she cried into the darkness.

****

Raisa felt the rushes of pleasure fill her and she screamed out. She sat up in bed in the middle of the night. Her body was covered with perspiration. She felt sated and cold at the same time. Only at these moments, after these dreams, which she did not know whether to call them sent from heaven or hell, did she truly feel alive. She shook her head in frustration and screamed again. She lay back down, staring at the ceiling. Breathing heavily still, she tried catching her breath after making love to a memory of a woman who still haunted her, even now, after all these years.

It had been almost ten years to the day that she had last touched Carolyn. She had fucked so many women that after a while she lost count and all the faces blended together. Raisa realized that in cursing Carolyn that day she had cursed herself as well. Only in dreams did Raisa feel pleasure. Only in her dream world did she allow a woman to touch her and possess her. She had fought loving Carolyn ten long years. It was enough, she finally told herself. She sat up and stared into the emptiness of her bedroom. She was alone. She finally acknowledged that it was by choice.

****

When Carolyn woke up in the morning she felt stiff. She stretched as if to bring to life a body that had been dormant for many years. For a moment she put out her hand to her eyes to block out the sunlight. She then looked around the room. Leaves were strewn everywhere. The marble floor seemed wet near the French doors, which were still wide open. Carolyn got up slowly and walked over to the welcoming sunshine coming from outside. She looked around her garden and was filled with newfound vigor. All was covered with the dew of a new morning. She could hear the singing of the birds and her nose was suddenly filled with the scent of roses.

"Mmmmmm…." She breathed in and closed her eyes in a comforting gesture. "The night is over. It's a new day."

****

The old woman held Raisa tightly to her and wept.   Raisa was immediately filled with guilt and regret.

"I'm sorry it's been so long, Nona." She held the old woman in a tight embrace as well.   "I've been busy…. I should have come sooner."

"How long can you stay this time?"   The old lady was looking into her eyes now.

"A few days, I can only stay a few days," Raisa said, sadly looking away.

"Come, let us sit in the shade for a while."

Raisa followed Nona to the verandah and sat next to her.

"Antonio bought some new horses.   You might like to see if there is one that might please you in the bunch."   Nona looked at her tentatively.

"No, I will just ride whatever when I come to visit.   There is no need for me to select an animal for myself."

"Raisa, you must forgive yourself for Furioso.   You must let that go," Nona said gently.

Raisa got up quickly and walked over to the railing.   She looked at the sights that once had given her so much joy and somehow, she realized, she had lost that feeling.   She no longer felt peaceful here.

"I killed him, Nona. He trusted me and I killed him." She spoke with no emotion.

"Raisa…"

"We can't lie to each other, you and I." Raisa turned and was now facing the old woman.   "I killed him."

Nona looked down unable to dispute the truthfulness of the words.   "You were not yourself in those days."

"That is no excuse.   He trusted me, loved me and I, with no regard, took his life because…" Raisa turned her back to the old woman unable or unwilling to continue.

Nona looked up now.   "If you speak about her perhaps the ghosts will leave you," the old woman said softly.   "Raisa…"

"No," Raisa simply said.

"Mi angel…"

"I don't want to have this conversation," Raisa stated firmly.

"Raisa, you have to let this anger go. It is making you…"

"Evil!" Raisa faced the old woman with a cold mask on her features.

"No, mi angel, you are not evil," the old woman said sadly.

"You are the only one who believes that." Raisa walked further down the verandah, then turned to face Nona again.

"I am getting old, Raisa. I want you to find some peace before I leave this world."

Raisa quickly closed the distance between them and knelt down in front of the old woman.

"Are you ill, Nona?"

The old woman smiled and caressed Raisa's face lovingly. "Not ill little one, just old."

Raisa put her head on the old woman's lap and as expected Nona caressed the dark tresses.

"I have missed you, little one," the old woman said softly as tears ran down her face. "You have let this anger live inside you too long. All your passion for life has turned into something else."

"You are all I have, Nona."

"You must allow yourself to love, Raisa. Or you will disappear one day. Mi angel, I won't always be here. I want you to allow yourself to love again."

"I don't want love. I don't need it" Raisa said curtly, getting up.

"Raisa!"

"No! People like me should just stay away from those sentiments. Have you forgotten it all? Don't make me into something that I'm not! Don't lie to yourself!"

"Raisa! Andrea's death was not your fault!" Nona said firmly.

"I should have been there. All he ever wanted to do was live here in his beloved Virago. He went into Copeco because of me, because of all that happened when…" she trailed off.

"After Carolyn left. Why don't you say her name and move on with your life?"

"Because I can't! Because she was my life, because....
Nothing mattered after she left me." Raisa turned her back to the
woman as her eyes began to fill with tears. "Because, when she left
I felt nothing. I ran Furioso to his death. I ...only thought of what I
wanted. Andreas came to Copeco because I wanted it. He died out
in that rig because I sent him." A sob escaped.

Nona walked up to her and held her tightly. Raisa tried to
pull away at first then just allowed herself to let go finally.

"All I know how to do is destroy, Nona. All that I ever
loved, I have destroyed." Raisa pulled away and stared out into the
forest. "I can't even feel anymore. I can't or I won't... I don't
know." She closed her eyes and at that moment Nona saw the years
that had passed show on her face.

"Mi angel..."

"I can't even be here at Virago."

"Andreas would have wanted..."

Raisa interrupted. "It's not Andreas!" She blurted out then
continued softly. "It's her. Don't you see, Nona, it's still her. I
never learned to live without her. I just exist."

"Then change your destiny."

"What?" Raisa turned and laughed. "Nona, it's been ten
years. It's too late."

"When your mother left..."

"I don't want to talk about..." Raisa interrupted only to be
interrupted by Nona

"You will listen! When your mother left she was hurt inside
and angry, mostly she was frightened. Martin was a lot like you."
Nona was looking at her very seriously now.

Raisa looked down.

"He should have gone after her. She loved him even then.
She would have come back."

Raisa stared at her in disbelief. "Come back to what? To
his anger, to this country that she hated, to those who loved her?"
Raisa stood in shock at what she had just said.

"Yes, to come back to those who loved her," Nona
confirmed softly. "She loved all of you. He shut her out because
she had hurt him. She was the only one that could and it was more

than he wanted to admit." Nona looked towards Raisa and noticed that she was really listening. "Adele would have come back. They were both too frightened and too proud."

Raisa stared at her now, questioning. Her eyes showed the insecurity and fear that she held inside her.

"You don't have to make the same mistakes. Change your destiny, Raisa, or you will be no better. You can start by picking out a horse tomorrow."

Raisa listened to the old woman. Encouraged by her silence Nona continued. "Ride around Virago. Allow yourself to find the peace it once gave you. And open up that room," Nona finished sadly. "Walk inside it and allow yourself to remember."

Nona kissed her on the cheek and left her. Raisa looked out into the lush jungle in front of her and wondered if perhaps she should try.

****

Later on that night, after dinner, Raisa took a walk around the house. Somehow, and without having planned it, she stood in front of the French doors that had been closed for almost ten years. She tried the doorknobs and was surprised to find that they turned easily. She opened them and walked inside the bedroom. It was spotlessly clean and yet all that had been left there that night was still in the same place. The dress she had worn that night was still over the chair. Small details to some but it gave Raisa a feeling like she had just been there only a few minutes ago.

Raisa walked over to the vanity and lightly touched the perfume bottle that she had given Carolyn.

She picked up the bottle, opened it and brought the snifter to her nose. As the scent filled her senses she finally said the name that she could not bear to hear out loud.

"Carolyn...Carolyn..." The tears that she had not shed seemed to come forth all of a sudden. "Carolyn..." She fell to her knees and cried into the night.

Chapter Twenty

"Mom…Mom?"

Carolyn sat in front of her desk staring out the window.

"Mom?" Simon called out again walking closer to her.

"Oh! Simon, I'm sorry, sweetheart. I was distracted." She smiled at her son and walked up to him and kissed him on the cheek. "How was school today?"

"Oh, you know. Mom, can we go to the mall later? I need to get something."

"What happened to your car?"

"Nothing, my car's fine. I thought you and I might eat something and maybe see a movie or something"

Carolyn smiled. "You thought that, huh?"

"Yeah, maybe we could do some shopping you know…. And maybe stop by a few stores."

"You want new clothes, huh?"

"Oh come on, mom." He said, laughing at having been caught.

"Okay, let me see if Amanda can have dinner with your grandparents."

"Sounds good. I'll leave my stuff upstairs and then we can take off."

"All right."

****

The mall was full of people as it usually was on a Friday afternoon. They had done some shopping and sat down near the food court. They finally decided to have a few things from different vendors and both mother and son began to eat their meal before going to see the movie they had finally agreed on.

"Mom?"

"What Simon?"

Simon looked at her sadly. "You do that a lot more now," he said simply.

"Do what, darling?"

"You kind of just leave."

"What are you talking about?" She asked while laughing.

"I'm older now, mom," he said to her.

Carolyn still looked at him not quite understanding what he was trying to stay.

"I knew about you and her," he said suddenly and looked down at his food now.

Carolyn just froze and stared at her son.

Simon looked up and saw the uncertainty in his mother's eyes.

"I always knew." He looked down at his food again. "I didn't understand a lot of things then."

"Simon, I don't understand." Carolyn was not sure exactly where this conversation was going or what it was that Simon was referring to.

"That night," he looked up at his mother then looked back down again, "I heard you and Raisa."

"What did you hear?" Carolyn could hear the shakiness in her voice.

"I heard it all. Then Dad came in and all that other stuff that happened..." he trailed off.

Carolyn held both her hands together in front of her. She locked her hands together to stop their shaking. Suddenly, Simon's hand was over hers. Carolyn looked up with tear filled eyes.

"I understand a lot more about stuff now, mom," he said sadly to her.

"Simon, I don't know what to say to you." Tears started rolling down her face.

"You started just drifting off like that when we came back here."

She stared at her son not quite understanding, yet trying to.

"You just look out somewhere and you leave."

"Simon, I'm sorry," Carolyn said softly, looking down at his hand still over hers.

"No, I'm the one who is sorry, mom."

"Honey, you…"

"I remember you tried talking to me when we went back to Caracas. I told you that if we didn't leave and we stayed there with her I would leave with my father."

"Simon, you were a child."

"Mom, I knew, okay?" He looked away feeling ashamed. "I knew, mom. I knew you wanted to go back to her. I knew."

"Simon," Carolyn said gently, "that was a long time ago. And I made the right choice."

Suddenly he seemed desperate to discuss this with her. "Maybe you can try to talk to her."

"No, that was a long time ago. And I left because I chose to, not because of anything you might have said. I don't want you to carry this guilt inside you. I chose Simon, I chose."

"Mom, I just want you to be happy. I know you're not. I was a stupid kid. I didn't want to see a lot of things then." He looked ashamed again. "If being with a woman is what makes you happy I want that for you."

"Oh Simon, that's is very good of you. But darling…"

"If you want to leave my father I will go with you mom and so will Amanda."

Carolyn looked surprised.

"I know you aren't happy. I know all the stuff that has happened all these years. I know about Amanda, too."

"Simon…"

"I won't ever tell her, I swear," Simon said quickly.

"Simon darling, I don't know what you think you know. But..."

"Mom, I remember you crying, telling her how he raped you."

Carolyn stared and saw the pain in her son's eyes.

"Simon..." She didn't know how to answer this or how to comfort him.

"I know about all the women and I know that he treats you like shit."

"Simon..."

"Sorry mom, I know you don't like me talking like that. But that's what he is."

"Simon..."

"I want you to be happy. I remember how you laughed when you were happy."

"Simon..." Carolyn allowed the tears to finally fall freely down her face.

"Let's go watch that movie." He squeezed her hands and smiled at her. "We can talk some more later, okay? I just wanted you to know that I want you to be happy. And I will go with you wherever that happiness may be, okay?"

Carolyn smiled at her son. "Okay, Simon. When did you grow up anyway?" She smiled as she asked.

"It kind of crept up on me," he said and they laughed together.

****

Raisa woke up lying on the floor. She fell asleep wallowing in her pain and feeling her inadequacy. She got up and walked out onto the open verandah and watched as the sun came over the horizon. She looked around Virago and tried to remember the inner peace she used to feel. So much had changed. No longer did she have Andreas to remind her of her humanity, and to believe in it.

And then she allowed herself to think of Furioso. How could

she have had such little regard?   Raisa took a deep breath. Perhaps Carolyn had been right. There was too much violence in her. She had killed that animal without a second thought. All she knew that day was that Carolyn was leaving and that she had to reach the plane before it took off with her. She had killed that fine and noble animal. She had thought of nothing but what she wanted. Raisa shook her head, trying to dispel the guilt she still carried within her.

Then there was Andreas. She was responsible for so much pain. At that moment she also came to terms with her violent nature and accepted it. She would not deny what and who she was anymore. There were times that she denied it like with Carolyn and times that she wrestled with it, God knows, Andreas had known that. And then there were the times that she just nullified her humanity and did whatever it took to win. Like with Copeco and all that had happened ten years ago. She had justified over and over again each and every death. And perhaps, it was just that she never felt any joy. How many had died so that her power and wealth would grow and surpass what any human being could ever need or want? She had fed her need to posses everything in sight thinking that if she accumulated enough power her other wants would disappear. They had not. Slowly, the cold had crept in and now she felt only the vast emptiness inside her.

Raisa looked out and silently prayed for a sign of something; some spark that would let her know that she was still alive. She was ashamed to admit she didn't even weep for Andreas anymore. The only time she felt anything was when she remembered Carolyn. Then, all she felt was pain and more pain. She had lost the ability to feel anything other than that.

Living had become choices of percentages. How much could be lost so that more was gained. How many people were expendable so that the company would thrive? It was all mathematics. Nothing was real. Life meant nothing. How could it? She had nothing to lose.

Chapter Twenty-One

Copeco had its annual meeting, as usual, in Dallas. All executives attended the week-long conferences. These were also the times when the redistricting of different areas was announced and transfers solidified. One obvious difference in this conference was that the CEO of Copeco would be attending the gala celebration. The office was buzzing with this news when Matt walked in that morning.

"What's all the excitement, Claire?" Matt leaned over with a bright smile. He had been trying to get Claire to go out with him for the last four months.

"All execs just got a memo that Ms. Andieta will be at the gala dinner this year. Your memo is on your desk."

Matt quickly went into his office and looked at the memo lying on the middle of his desk. Raisa was coming. He knew that one day this would happen. He told himself over and over again to play it cool.

"Matt, did you know she was coming?" Claire asked from behind him.

"Naturally, but I couldn't say anything." Matt turned around with his confident smile.

"Do you know when she is actually coming in?"

"I'm sorry, Claire, I really can't say. Raisa is a very private person."

"Oh, of course. Will you introduce me?" Claire was hanging on his every word.

"If that's what would please you, yes, of course." Matt smiled devilishly.

"And who am I supposed to be meeting?" A voice from the door made them both turn around.

Matt froze instantly.

"May I help you?" Claire walked up to the dark haired woman in front of her.

"Claire!" Matt held her back by the arm. "This is Ms. Raisa Andieta."

Claire, surprised for a moment, began to babble. "Oh Ms. Andieta, it's such a pleasure to finally meet you. I've read the articles about you in *Money Magazine* and the one in *Fortune 500* last month. It's such a pleasure to meet you," she continued shaking Raisa's hand.

"Yes, I can see that," she said soberly, looking at Matt. Matt immediately intervened.

"You must let go of her hand now, Claire."

Claire looked embarrassed. "Oh, I'm sorry. Matt has told me so much about you."

"Has he now," Raisa said with a sardonic smile. "All good I hope, Matt?"

"Of course, of course." Matt laughed but Raisa could see him beginning to sweat.

"Now, if you don't mind I would like a few minutes with Mr. Stenbeck," Raisa said as she walked into the office and sat down behind Matt's desk.

Claire looked at Matt uncomfortably and left, the office closing the door behind her.

"Sit down, please," Raisa purred.

Matt sat down without uttering a word.

"I plan to attend the gala this year, to hand out the promotions and so on. I am making some changes in management and I want to see all the execs. First hand. I will, of course, count on your advice and guidance."

There, he said to himself. She had given him a way of saving face. Matt nodded his head and accepted the offering. Their pact was still intact.

****

"Amanda, you simply cannot do things your way just because you want to!" Carolyn said to the child, trying to contain the anger in her voice.

"Ms. Wasneski is an idiot!" The child turned her face away from her mother defiantly.

"Amanda!"

"Well, she is, Mom! She babbles on and on about things that are absolutely ridiculous. I asked her a real question and she said I was insolent because she didn't know the answer. I know that's why," the child blurted out.

"Amanda darling, you can't keep on with this behavior. I know that history is a subject that you love but, sometimes you have to focus on what's expected in class and do more on your own." Carolyn tried to sound reasonable.

"I thought that school was for learning." Amanda pouted in defiance.

"Yes, school **is** for learning. It's also so that we may learn to deal with people. You can't always challenge people, Mandy...most will push back."

"Hmmm."

"You have to learn that some things are just not acceptable. I know that you are a very intelligent girl. I know that. Your teacher knows that. But, it doesn't give you the right to make fun of others."

"I don't do that, mom," she said, looking ashamed now.

"We have to watch what we say, darling. Sometimes words really hurt."

The child looked out the car window and really thought about what her mother said. She looked towards her mother again. "When someone says awful things it means that they don't like you."

"Yes."

The child looked at her mother awhile longer, then stared out the car window once more without saying another word.

121

****

Raisa walked into the boardroom. All of the executives of Copeco in Dallas were present. She gave them detailed information as to what she expected to happen in the upcoming, one-week conference for Copeco.

Suddenly, the agenda to the conference was changed but no one voiced a protest. All knew better than to challenge Raisa Andieta. Her temper and her retaliation to opposition was legendary.

Everyone left the boardroom with unpleasant looks on their faces. All of a sudden they had to plan a whole new conference within two days. Matt was the only one whose feathers seemed unruffled. Her presence in the boardroom and her referring to him had established the pecking order early in the game. All knew that he was her right hand man.

As everyone left them alone, Matt made the invitation he dreaded making. "Ms. Andieta, if you are not busy this evening I would like to invite you to dinner."

"At your house?" Her comeback was quick.

"Yes, if you like, of course," he immediately added, being thrown off course.

"Thank you, but no. This trip won't be a long one and I have pressing business to see to in Europe." She dismissed him with just a look.

He got up and walked out with a sigh of relief.

****

The next day things still seemed to be on overdrive for Carolyn. She had woken up with a restlessness that she had not felt for a long time. That afternoon, the kids came home and rushed upstairs before she could see them. She followed them, a sinking feeling in her stomach.

122

"Mom, it's not as bad as it seems," Simon said to his mother as she walked in further into the room

"Oh my God!" Carolyn gasped.

"He hit me first!" Amanda exclaimed.

Carolyn looked at Simon who looked elsewhere.

"Amanda, you have a black eye! What happened?" Carolyn asked as she was trying to gage her daughter's injury.

"Jarred is a pain. He is always going on and on about how much better boys are than girls."

"And?"

"I told him he was a girl!"

"Amanda!"

"He swung at me, and missed so I slugged him!" She said proudly.

"How did you get this black eye?"

"His two other friends started fighting too."

"But…"

The phone rang and Carolyn went to answer it signaling her children to wait.

"Hello?"

There was a moment of silence.

"Yes, Ms. Wasneski, I am talking to her right now…No, I didn't hear that… Of course I will talk to her…Yes…. Tomorrow at nine AM is fine…Thank you for calling me."

Carolyn turned around to face her daughter again.

"Oh-oh, I think she knows, Mandy," Simon said under his breath.

"What did you do to the computer lab?"

****

That night, all four members of the family were seated around the dinner table. And, as usual, all ate quietly.

"What happened to your eye?" Matt sounded annoyed, also as

123

usual.

"I was in a fight in school," Amanda answered.

Matt looked at Carolyn. "We have a conference tomorrow at nine AM at her school. They want us both to come."

"I can't."

"Matt, this is important."

"I can't, the whole office is in an uproar. Raisa Andieta will be attending the conference and gala this year and she has changed the whole program."

"Raisa is here?" Carolyn said before she could stop herself.

"Yes, she got here yesterday. And with her usual finesse she has us all in an uproar," Matt said curtly, put his napkin down and left the room.

Carolyn got up as well and followed him out the door and into the grand room.

"Matt, I really wish you would try to make this meeting tomorrow. Amanda is out of control. I want you to actively participate here!" Her irritation finally got his attention.

"Carolyn, you always deal with the children, you know that," he said exasperated.

"She's getting into trouble all the time, Matt, I don't know what to do or how to reason with her. Perhaps if you…"

"Oh no! Don't lay this guilt trip on me!"

"I'm not, but she is our daughter. We have to try and make some sense out of this behavior before it becomes more destructive. She's getting into fights, she's acting up in class; Matt, I need your help."

"I would know how to deal with her if she were a boy."

"How? Like Simon? You barely give him the time of day." Carolyn was really angry now.

"He is more like you than me!"

"And Amanda? What's your excuse with Amanda?"

"If I didn't know any better…"

"What? What!"

"It's a joke, isn't it?"

"What are you going on about, Matt?" Carolyn asked in frustration.

"Amanda, if it were at all possible I would say she was Raisa Andieta's bastard!"

Carolyn stared at him in disbelief. They had never openly discussed this. She visibly paled.

"You think I didn't put two and two together? All that bitch needs is a cock!" He growled at her.

"She doesn't need one, Matt." With that, Carolyn walked out of the room and left Matt speechless.

****

Carolyn walked out of the room only to bump straight into her children, who both stood in front of her, horrified. Carolyn wanted the ground to open up and swallow her whole.

"Mommy? Why doesn't Daddy love me?"

Carolyn knelt down in front of her daughter. She tried touching her, but the child pulled away. "Who is Raisa Andieta?"

Carolyn stared unable to speak.

"Mandy..." Simon knelt in front of her. "You know Dad says some real dumb things sometimes?" He was being so gentle with her.

"He said that I was her bastard!"

"No, darling, that's not what he said." Carolyn again tried reaching for her daughter.

"I don't understand!" Amanda screamed.

Amanda ran and Simon went after her. Carolyn's world was whirling out of her hands. She took a deep breath to control herself and then turned to go after the children to see how much damage had occurred.

At that very moment Matt came out of the room. "What's the ruckus?"

"Amanda heard us arguing. She heard what you said."

"Well, I have a lot of work to do tonight for this conference, keep her quiet Carolyn."

125

With that Carolyn lost what little control she had left.

"You conceited son of a bitch!" She went to slap him and he caught her arm, pushing her away.

"As usual, you are getting overly emotional," he merely said as he tried to straighten his jacket.

"Don't you care about them at all, Matt? Was I so blind? Have you always been this callous asshole?"

They both stood, looking at each other. Matt broke the eye contact first. "I'm sorry she overheard." He walked to his office, never looking back, and locked the door behind him.

Carolyn's hand shook as she brought it up to her face. She felt flushed. She immediately turned around and went after Simon and Amanda.

Chapter Twenty-Two

Half way through the conferences, Matt found out that the European position might become available within the upcoming year. He remembered that Raisa had mentioned that she had pressing business in Europe. If he played his cards right that much-sought-after position might be his.

"Matt!"

Matt turned around and saw the general manager of Rig 54, Harry Pentak, approaching.

"Hello Harry," Matt said as they shook hands.

"Have you heard?" Harry said below his breath.

"Heard?"

"Most of the general managers would support you if you go for it. I want to remind you that I'm the president of that association."

"Thank you, Harry" Matt said with a big smile. "I always remember my friends."

"I know you take care of your people, Matt. I just wanted to let you know that we would support you just in case you need the muscle."

"Thanks Harry, I have an ace myself."

"I know that you are supposed to be tight with Ms. Ice herself, but if the others…."

"One thing I learned a long time ago: Whatever she says goes.

None of those pricks would even try to cross her." Matt laughed heartily.

****

The final day of the conference was long and tedious so all were looking forward to the Gala. All of Dallas showed up with all their finery. Most of the Who's Who that had something to do with the oil business and the cream of that crop worked for Copeco.

Raisa sat back and watched as the men in their tuxedos strolled around with cowboy boots and 10-gallon hats, while the women wore the most outrageous gowns only to be outdone by the jewelry they displayed on their bodies. She went through the motions of giving her speech and handing out special mentions and awards, all the time scanning the room waiting.... waiting, but not wanting to admit who she was waiting for.

Finally, she spotted Matt, who walked in alone. Men and women immediately surrounded him. Carolyn was not with him.

Raisa decided that she was tired. They could finish this party without her. She said her good-byes to the governor and left the Gala accompanied by her two bodyguards.

Matt had been late. He was supposed to have been there to do some of the presentations with her. The audacity of the man was beyond reason. All the antipathy she felt for him suddenly surfaced as she got into the private elevator that would take her straight to the penthouse.

When she entered her floor she immediately saw a situation unfolding before her.

A young man started walking towards her and was blocked by one of her bodyguards. The young man was thrown down to the floor.

"What in hell is going on here?" Raisa demanded.

"We caught him trying to sneak into your rooms, Ms. Andieta. We will take care of this" One of the men who was supposed to be on security detail on her floor spoke.

"Wait! Raisa! It's Simon," the boy said with his face against the carpet.

"Get off him! Now!"

They released Simon and he slowly got up.

Suddenly before her was a young man. No longer the boy that she remembered. He towered over her. And her inspection suddenly stopped at his eyes.

"You have your mother's eyes."

"Yeah," he said with a floppy smile.

"Are you all right? Did they hurt you?" Raisa asked, as she looked him over.

"I'm sorry, Ms. Andieta, but he…"

She cut in immediately. "It's not bad enough that you wrestled a boy to the ground but you are going to give me excuses?"

"No Ma'am, that's not…."

"Good, now go do your job. How did you get up here?" She looked towards Simon who answered proudly.

"I got in through the service elevator," he added with a smile. Raisa could not hide her smile either.

"Come in, Simon." She led him into the main room of the Penthouse. "Would you like something to drink?"

"No, no thank you." He walked around. "Wow, this is some place." He walked up to the glass wall and saw all of Dallas in front of him. "Wow, what a view!"

"Yes." Raisa watched him as he moved around the room. He was a part of Carolyn, her mind kept telling her over and over again and he was here. "Why are you here, Simon?" She asked as she sat down on the sofa and crossed her legs.

He turned around, walked over to a chair close to her and sat down. He seemed to be trying to find the words.

"Did your mother send you?"

"No!" His head suddenly came up. "She doesn't know I'm here."

Raisa waited. The boy took a long breath and then it all seemed to pour out of him.

"My mother is not happy. I know that you loved her once. Things between her and my father were never good but I thought…I know that I was to blame for her leaving and coming back here."

"Simon…"

He did not let her speak. "I know that you two were…" He looked down to the floor. And Raisa said nothing. "I know that she loved you. I didn't understand then. She was so happy…. I want to know if you still love her."

Raisa never expected this. She got up and walked towards the glass wall in front of her. She spoke softly, her back towards Simon.

"That was a long time ago, Simon."

"My father doesn't deserve her."

"She chose him."

"I told her I wouldn't stay with her if she stayed." As soon as he said it she turned to face him. He looked ashamed and it showed on his young face. "She wanted to stay."

Raisa took a deep breath before speaking. This whole night had been something she had not expected. "It was a long time ago, Simon. We were both young. It's been ten years."

"I know she still loves you."

"Simon, I don't think we should be discussing your mother like this." She tried to put some distance between them.

"If you love her…"

"It's not always enough."

He looked at her and said nothing. She began to feel uncomfortable under his speculative eyes.

"I love my mother. He doesn't. I know now he never has. I don't know if he loves anyone beside himself. He takes a little part of her away almost every day. One day…. she will just disappear. At least I'm fighting for her. Amanda is just fighting. I thought that real love never dies?"

Raisa looked at him without so much as breathing. He walked up to her and kissed her lightly on the cheek. "That's for being so good to me when we were at Virago. I never thanked you." He turned around and slowly walked out.

She walked again towards the glass wall. She looked on and saw all the lights before her. And in the reflection of the dark glass a tear could be seen escaping her eye as it slowly slipped down her face.

****

The next day she was packed up and sitting in first class on her way back to Venezuela. She was going home. Europe would have to wait.

Suddenly her cell phone rang. "Oigo?" She became visibly pale.

"Have a jet fueled and ready for me at the airport" Raisa watched as her hands began to shake. Her life was coming full circle.

****

She arrived at Virago and ran up the steps. No one had to tell her how grave the situation was; she could see it in their faces. Raisa went directly to the Nona's room

"Nona!" She knelt down next to the bed.

"I've been waiting for you. I knew you would come." Raisa could see that the eyes seemed dull and not even her smile held that usual vibrancy.

"You have been very naughty, I should be angry with you," Raisa said softly.

"No, don't be angry, mi angel, I didn't want to worry you." The old woman spoke with difficulty

Raisa smiled and looked down as her hand covered Nona's. She suddenly noticed how the old woman's hand was frail and thin. She looked up again and all the fear that lay in her showed in her eyes.

"You must fight for your happiness. I know that there is so much love inside you, mi angel." Nona's hand reached out and caressed the face that she had loved so dearly. She had given Raisa all of the tenderness and love she had once given her own daughter before she had died. She would do all that was possible to get this, the child closest to her heart, to find joy at last.

"All I need is you," Raisa was barely able to say as tears ran freely down her face.

"Pick a horse for my sake and ride him. Open your heart. You have one, even if you do try to hide it. And it's a strong heart. A good heart."

"Nona…"

"You will go on and you will do this for me." The old woman's eyes filled with tears as well. "From the first day I saw you, I loved you. You cried with all the vigor of life inside you. Be who you are. Be my strong and brave little soldier. It is a role that suits you. You have fought your whole life. Now, you must fight for your happiness."

"Don't go. Please stay with me," she cried as her face went down and touched the old woman's hand.

Nona caressed the dark tresses lovingly as she always had. "I will always be with you. Mi angel…love never dies. Remember that; love never dies."

Raisa's face lay on that hand as her tears came of their own volition. She felt when the caresses to her hair stopped. And, at that moment, she knew.

She never raised her head as sobs racked her body.

Chapter Twenty-Three

This unfeelingness seemed to fit her like a glove. It had been three weeks since Nona had been buried. Raisa still wore mourning colors. But, unlike other times, she had not run; this time she had stayed. She walked around the whole hacienda everyday.

All the old servants who had recognized her devotion to the old woman looked at her in sadness. They saw the pain in her eyes that she thought was so well hidden. They doted on her and even went out of their way to make her favorite dishes but even so, most of the time the dishes returned to the kitchen barely touched.

Raisa had gotten thinner and to anyone who looked at her she simply looked more chiseled in features. But, then again, who really knew her? If they only knew that the once feared and powerful woman cried herself to sleep every night. Or that she slept sitting in a chair because she could not bear the memories of the woman she loved and who had once shared that bed. And yet, she had stayed in Virago and she returned to her old bedroom each and every night.

As she walked one day it suddenly occurred to her that all that she had ever really and truly loved had been at Virago. All that had shaped her, hurt her or meant anything to her, had been or come from there. She looked around, and almost at that same instant, the lush greenery that surrounded her seemed to be alive. A breeze like many a long time ago came slowly and caressed her starved skin. She inhaled the sweetness of the earth beneath her and she felt the power of this land as it called out to her once more.

She closed her eyes as they filled with tears and, as she opened them, she was filled with a longing she could no longer deny. She had asked for a sign and when it came she had not seen it. And now this place that was her life force had once again made it all clear to her. It was so simple. Love never dies.

Raisa looked around once more and walked in a rush to the stables.

"Tomas?"

"I'm here."

"Good, are those the new horses?"

"Yes."

"Come," she said simply and the ranch hand followed.

She leaned against the fence and looked as the horses ran around and played. After a few minutes she saw it. It was a bay with sharp eyes. The horse seemed arrogant and she recognized it as spirit. She pointed to it.

"Separate that mare from the rest and put her in my stall. Order a name plate for her."

Tomas smiled "What shall I put on it?"

She looked at him and a sad smile appeared as she said. "Esperanza."

The name hope seemed appropriate. She looked at the horse once more and headed back to the main house.

****

Four days later Raisa arrived at Dallas International Airport. Arrangements had been made and a car waited for her. She was rushed through customs. The limousine took her to the penthouse she always stayed in when she came to Dallas. It was one of Copeco's many properties. Within hours, she had made sure to touch base with her office in Caracas and instructed all inquiries to be rerouted to Dallas.

That night Raisa stood in front of the glass wall in front of her, looked at all those lights and, as she took a deep breath, she turned around and went to bed. As she lay her head down all that kept going through her head was the word....*Tomorrow*.

****

"I don't know why you just don't send her in the car," Matt said in exasperation.

"I enjoy driving her to school, Matt."

"Did it ever occur to you that she is over indulged? Maybe that's why she is having these temper tantrums."

"You know one day you are going to actually say something intelligent and I am going to miss it," Carolyn said as she picked up the keys and left him with his coffee cup half way to his mouth.

Carolyn could see that Amanda had just gotten into the car. She walked over to the driver's side and got in.

"Ready, Sweetheart?"

"Yes." She kept looking out the window.

Carolyn sat and watched her daughter who had almost stopped looking at her straight in the eyes these days. Slowly she was losing Mandy and she knew it.   She just didn't know how to stop it.

Carolyn caressed the dark tresses of hair and the child turned around to face her. For one brief moment she saw such fear in those eyes.

"Amanda..."

"We are going to be late, mom." The child once again turned to look out the window.

"Amanda, what's wrong baby? I can't help you if you won't talk to me," she said softly.

"Nothing's wrong, mom."

"It hurts, Amanda," Carolyn said and as her voice faltered the child looked at her again. "It hurts me that you can't talk to me."

"If I ask you something, will you tell me the truth?"   The child finally spoke while looking at her mother intently.

Carolyn thought for a moment then looked up and nodded her head.

"Are you my real mother?"

Carolyn's face showed her surprise. "Yes, of course I am."

"I don't look like you or Daddy."

"You look like my father's family, sweetheart. They have dark hair and blue eyes like yours." She tenderly caressed the soft cheek of her child. "You are my own beautiful little girl."

Amanda looked at her hard and long and finally, Carolyn could see the change and realized that she had believed her.

"Can I ask you one more thing?"

"Yes."

"Who is Raisa Andieta?"

Carolyn did not hesitate in her answer. "Someone I knew a long time ago."

"Daddy didn't like her did he?"

"No," Carolyn said sadly.

"Okay."

****

Carolyn dropped Amanda off at school and started with her usual errands. It was Monday and on Mondays she picked up fresh flowers and went to her favorite little café for coffee next door to the flower shop.

As she was walking out of the florist shop she came to a sudden stop.

"Hello," said Raisa gently. "Can I help you with those?"

"Oh, um…" she seemed to be juggling the bouquet.

"Here, you hold on to those and I'll take these." Raisa took possession of some of the blooms. "Is your car close by?"

"Yes, I'm parked right there" Carolyn answered in a daze.

Both women walked quietly. Carolyn opened the car and placed the flowers inside the back of her car and then closed the hatch. She turned around and again was faced with a memory from long ago.

Raisa smiled. "I've heard that place makes great coffee," she said as she pointed to the very shop that Carolyn was heading to before.

"Yes, yes it does." She felt awkward and infantile.

"Would you have some with me?" Raisa asked simply.

Carolyn thought a moment and then her answer was "Yes."

Both walked in unison. Neither was daring to speak for fear of saying something wrong. Raisa pulled the door open and Carolyn entered. They both automatically went to Carolyn's usual table. Carolyn smiled to herself. The cappuccinos were delicious.

"How long have you been in Dallas?" Carolyn finally spoke

"Only a few days."

"Matt didn't say anything," Carolyn said looking away.

"Matt doesn't know."

Carolyn looked at Raisa again. Raisa began to drink her coffee once more.

"Do you like it?"

"Yes." Raisa met her eyes again with a smile and was rewarded by one in return.

"Will you be here long?"

"I'm not sure."

Carolyn knew when Raisa was being evasive so she decided to change the subject.

"How is Andreas?" Almost immediately she saw the pain register in Raisa's face.

"He died eight years ago" Raisa answered looking down at her coffee cup.

Carolyn's hand covered hers. When Raisa looked up, Carolyn could see the tears welling up behind the eyes that once had said so much to her.

"I'm sorry," Carolyn said sadly. "I'm so sorry."

Raisa looked back down and her other hand began to caress the hand that Carolyn had placed over hers. *Such a simple thing,* Raisa said to herself, *and such comfort by the mere touch of her hand.*

"Love never dies," Raisa finally said out loud.

"No, it doesn't," Carolyn replied and as she did Raisa's eyes met hers once more. "How did it happen?"

Raisa removed her hands and began to fidget. Carolyn yearned for the warmth as soon as it had been lost and suddenly she saw so much of Raisa in Amanda. The withdrawal and the tenseness, the fidgeting and the raw emotions.

"Out on a rig," Raisa answered looking out the window.

"I'm sorry," Carolyn said sadly.

"He should never have been out there," Raisa replied without looking at Carolyn again.

"I'm glad I got to meet him.   Andreas was a very special man."

"Yes, yes he was." She paused for a moment then became all business like.   "He left a son behind."

"He was married?" Carolyn asked with a smile.

"No, he was not." She did not offer any more explanation.

Carolyn said nothing and Raisa faced her once more.

"She took his money and left him his son," Raisa said bitterly. "She killed a part of him.   I killed the rest."

Carolyn stared and could see the old anger poking its head again.

"Raisa..." Carolyn felt her heart go out to the beautiful woman in front of her who tried so hard to be strong and whose pain came through so clearly.

"I'm sorry, I'm running late.   It was nice seeing you again," Raisa said as she quickly got up to leave.

Carolyn said nothing as she walked away.

****

Carolyn drove around all day, aimlessly. She was bombarded with an onslaught of emotions.   Raisa brought, in some ways, a ray of her forgotten vigor and youth.   Raisa, of course, had also brought back other memories.   And along with all the good came the bad. Carolyn once again had felt first hand her moodiness and her inability to face...and suddenly Carolyn saw it clearly.   Raisa didn't run from love.   She never had.   Raisa had always fought for it and rejoiced in it.   Raisa ran from being loved.   Being loved frightened her.   Because then Raisa would be faced with the possibility of hurting someone she cared for. In her own way Raisa thought that if they didn't love you, they couldn't hurt you.

Carolyn stopped in front of her garage and just let her head fall back. She raised her head as the truth was finally revealed after all this time. Raisa had been afraid of her.

Carolyn had always mistaken her bravado and her passion for aggression. And it had been neither. It had been her need to pull what she wanted to her. It had been her need to hold what was precious to her. It had always been the fear of loss. She had lost all that she had loved. Thank God she still had Nona, Carolyn told herself. Otherwise, once having known the passionate woman, her pain would be unbearable.

****

Carolyn walked into a full-blown war.

"Don't talk to her like that!" Simon screamed.

"What's going on here?" Carolyn asked as she walked into the room.

"Your daughter has struck again!" Matt yelled

Amanda was looking at the floor while seated in a nearby chair.

"What happened?" Carolyn asked.

"She was in another fight today," Simon said.

"Maybe you should buy her only pants from now on since she can't seem to behave like a proper young lady!" Matt bellowed.

"Matt!"

"Where were you? I tried calling you all afternoon. They pulled me out of a meeting to pick her up at school!"

"Amanda, are you all right?" Carolyn asked her daughter who still said nothing.

"Of course she's all right, she can slug it out with the best of em. She's a regular boy these days."

"Matt! Shut up!" Carolyn spat out.

"Don't you dare talk to me like that!" He went towards her.

"If you touch my mother, I'll kill you!" Simon jumped in front of him.

"Who the hell do you think you are?" Matt acted indignant, grabbing Simon roughly.

"Let go of him, Matt! Don't you dare touch him!" Carolyn pulled at Matt's arm and Amanda jumped up and started hitting her father.

Amanda kept punching and punching. Carolyn pulled her away and held her tightly as the child threw a fit and then, without warning, began to sob in her mother's embrace as they both sat on the floor.

Matt stared and Simon sat down and covered his face.

Carolyn caressed her hair and rocked the child in her arms back and forth. "It's all right, baby. Everything is going to be all right."

Matt slammed the door on his way out. Carolyn looked up and saw the pain in Simon's eyes as hers filled with tears. He came and sat down next to her.

****

Matt stormed into his office. "Claire!"

"Yes Matt, I'm here." Claire came in quickly.

"What's this?" He demanded.

"Those changes just came through."

"Who approved these changes in personnel?"

"I did," Raisa said standing at the doorway. "Do you usually get to the office at 2 in the afternoon or is today a special case?"

Claire wanted to disappear into the wallpaper, but Matt looked unnerved.

"There was a problem with my daughter at school."

Raisa inwardly faltered. "Is she all right?"

"She seems to attract trouble," he said with disdain.

"Spirited?"

"She will have to learn," he said to her in a challenge.

She seemed unfazed when she answered before walking

140

away. "Some of us never do."

"Bitch," Matt said under his breath.

Claire looked to see if Raisa might have overheard and took a deep breath of relief when she kept walking.

"Matt…"

"Claire, do you know why she's here?"

"Memo on your desk. The totem pole is being shook. She has taken over that big office on the 11th floor."

"Shit! Shit! Shit!" He spat, grabbed a glass holder on his desk and threw it against the wall.

Claire stared in horror. Matt sat down behind his desk and turned his chair to stare out the window.

Claire left the office and closed the door behind her as quietly as possible.

****

That afternoon Matt marched straight up to the 11th floor. He had been summoned.

"Come in, Matt," Raisa said as she kept reading the papers in front of her.

Matt sat down, not too happy.

She looked up. "Do you want the European seat?"

Matt had expected a fight and he was instead being offered a prize. His mouth hung open in stunned surprise.

"Should I consider your silence a yes?" She asked as she looked back down at her papers in boredom.

"Yes! Raisa, I don't know what to say. I never expected…"

"Don't say anything to anyone yet. Give me a week," she said as she looked up again.

"Of course, I understand. Thank you, Raisa." He was drooling all over himself with joy.

"Well, then consider it done. I'm busy, Matt, we'll talk later."

He had been dismissed. He got up and walked out the door in utter, joyful shock.

Chapter Twenty-Three

Copeco sponsored many community events in Dallas. This particular event was horsemanship. These were some of the things that Raisa enjoyed participating in. This event in particular was a competition of sorts for children from 8-10 for horsemanship and jumping. Since her arrival, she had noticed several good riders. Before the next round she decided to go down to the paddock and see some of the young riders and the horses they were competing with.

All the riders competed with numbers. It had always been done this way so as to promote non-favoritism. She remembered that she had really liked how well rider number nine had done.

When she saw the child with that number on their back she naturally walked there first.

"Hi," Raisa said as she approached.

"Hi."

"You were really very good today," Raisa praised.

"Thanks, but I almost hit the top pole that last jump." The child removed her helmet and dark hair covered her shoulders.

"You should pin that back." Raisa smiled and pointed at her hair.

"Yeah, I know but I sweat more that way."

"I used to let mine loose, too." Raisa conceded with a smile.

Amanda was intrigued and smiled back. "Do you ride?"

"I have done my share. I have quite a few ribbons to show for my bumps and bruises." Raisa smiled broadly.

"Can you give me some pointers about that last jump?"

"Well, actually, yes..."

The two compared notes and laughed a few times in unison.

Simon was walking towards the paddocks when he suddenly stopped, a smile covering his face. He turned around and walked the other way.

****

Carolyn sat on the bleachers and the riders began to get in order of participation. Number nine came out of the gate with gusto. Carolyn noticed the difference in posture immediately. Amanda seemed to come to life on the horse. She seemed to be taking more chances with her routine and she had sped up her jumps. Carolyn instinctively knew something had changed. On the last jump, Amanda barely managed to hang on and as she finished the jump the young rider fell off.

Carolyn started running instantly. A few other people jumped the fences and ran towards the field as well.

Raisa reached the young girl first since she had been watching from close by.

"Hey kid, you okay?" She touched the child gently.

Amanda turned around and tried to sit. "Yeah, I think so."

Two of the officials arrived next, and suddenly, Carolyn appeared on the ground kneeling next to her.

"Mandy baby, don't move." Carolyn was shaking visibly. "Let's wait for the doctor."

"Breathe deeply. Can you feel anything hurting?" Raisa asked as she outwardly checked Amanda's limbs.

Amanda shook her head.

"I think she's okay. Got the wind knocked out of her, that's all." Carolyn looked at the voice that had just spoken and only now saw Raisa beside her.

"Yeah mom, I'm okay. I just couldn't move for a minute there," the child said bravely.

"The doctor is on his way," one of the officials said.

"She's fine," Raisa assured.

"You don't know that!" Carolyn was getting angry.

"Let it go, Carolyn," Raisa said as quietly as possible.

"No! She is my child and you are not a doctor!"

"Mom, I'm okay!" Amanda said trying to get up, getting agitated and aggressive.

The doctor arrived and began to examine her.

"Leave me alone!" Amanda yelled.

"Amanda!" Carolyn tried to cajole her.

Raisa stood up to her full height. "Amanda, get up." All looked up at the imperious voice. Amanda stopped fidgeting and stood up. "Your gate was strong but you lost control of your horse because you didn't concentrate at the last jump."

Amanda nodded her head somberly.

"We will work on that," Raisa said as she placed her hand on the girl's shoulder. "Now, let the doctor check you over and then take care of your horse. He is your responsibility."

The child turned toward the doctor quietly. Carolyn was both in awe and furious.

They all walked to the medical tent and once the doctor was sure that the girl was fit Carolyn began to breathe easier.

Amanda went looking for Astro, her horse. Both she and Carolyn spotted Raisa brushing him as they approached.

Raisa looked up and she could tell that she was about to hear it.

"You told her to change her routine!" Carolyn didn't miss a breath. "How dare you interfere! She could have been killed!"

"No, she is a good rider. She is a strong rider too," Raisa said defensively.

"Mom..."

"You just come in and do what you please, don't you? You never stop to think of the what if," Carolyn said accusingly.

"Mom..."

"I told her to just be herself. You can't hide who you are, Carolyn!" Raisa attacked back.

"How dare you presume to tell me how to deal with my daughter!"

"Mom…"

"You were embarrassing her out there!"

"You pompous ass!"

"I would never have let her move if I thought that she might be hurt," Raisa said defensively.

"You are always right, aren't you?" Carolyn spat

"Carolyn, you are suffocating her!"

"How dare you tell me how to be a mother!"

Raisa took two steps back. "You are right, I don't know anything about mothers," Raisa said softly. Carolyn immediately felt the impact of her words.

"I'm okay, Mom," Amanda said as she put her arms around Carolyn's waist.

Carolyn looked down at the dark head and her hand began to caress it. Raisa looked on as if she were mesmerized.

Carolyn knelt down in front of her daughter and caressed the soft face of her little girl. "I love you, Amanda. If anything ever happened to you it would kill me." Tears ran down her face. "I want you to be strong and brave but you must take care because there are people who love you."

Carolyn stood up and looked at her daughter. Amanda went into her arms. Carolyn looked up and saw the tenderness she knew so well in the blue eyes, now before her. "Raisa…. I"

"I shouldn't have changed the routine without checking with her parents…. you, in this case….I didn't know she was yours," Raisa said with a sad smile. Her hand reached out to touch the child's hair as well but pulled back before doing so. Carolyn did not miss the attempt. "She's exquisite," Raisa said as her eyes sought the eyes of the woman in front of her.

Amanda pulled away from her mother and now stared at the woman in front of her in curiosity.

"Are you Raisa Andieta?" Amanda got both women's attention now.

"Yes, I am," Raisa answered the child.

"I'm supposed to be like you," Amanda said seriously, not breaking eye contact with Raisa.

Raisa looked at Carolyn.

"My father doesn't like you," Amanda stated.

"No, he doesn't," Raisa answered the child honestly, looking at her again.

Amanda looked at her speculatively for awhile. "He doesn't like me much either."

Carolyn thought her heart would break. She was about to say something before Raisa knelt down in front of the child in front of her.

"Sometimes, people don't understand," Raisa said gently and then gave her a smile. Amanda nodded in agreement.

Raisa reached out and put a lock of hair in front of the child's face behind her ear. "I used to.... your mother has a rebellious lock like yours."

Raisa got up and faced Carolyn now. Amanda put her hand inside Raisa's and her other hand in her mothers. Both women stood looking at the child and then at each other.

Carolyn looked down at her daughter and smiled. "Ice cream?"

Amanda nodded her head with a smile and looked at Raisa.

"Kid, have you ever tried mango ice cream?"

"Nope."

"Well, I have a surprise for you," Raisa and Amanda started walking without her. Carolyn laughed as she caught up with them.

Chapter Twenty-Four

"Hey! Where were you two?" Simon waltzed into the family room later that night. "We looked for you after the competition."

"How is George and Tim?" asked Carolyn, looking up from her book.

"Good, we had a blast. The new arcade is incredible." Simon sat down and looked at Amanda. "Hey squirt, how was your competition?"

"I fell but I learned lots," Amanda said seriously. Matt had been reading the newspaper and put it down at that moment.

"Yeah? Did it hurt?"

"Nah, just got the wind knocked out of me."

"Cool," Simon said "I went to see you but you were busy talking to Raisa so I...." Simon looked towards Matt and realized, too late, his mistake.

"Raisa was at the competition?" Matt directed his question to Carolyn.

"We had mango ice cream," Amanda interjected.

"You had ice cream with her?" Matt said with exasperation at his daughter.

"Me and Mom."

Simon looked at his mother and saw the tenseness in her building.

"Why didn't you tell me!" Matt exclaimed standing up and

looking straight at Carolyn.

"And I liked her," Amanda added insolently.

"You go to your room!" Matt pointed towards the door.

"Matt! What's wrong with you?"

"I liked her a lot! I liked her better than you!" Amanda spat out at him.

Matt became furious. "Go!"

Amanda got up and slammed the door behind her.

"What is wrong with you?" Carolyn immediately demanded in disbelief.

"Simon, leave!" Matt growled.

"No!" Simon refused.

"Simon, sweetheart, please. I want to speak with your father." Carolyn wanted to remove her son from Matt's anger.

Simon looked at his father then at his mother again and walked out of the room.

"What were you doing with Raisa today and with my daughter?"

"Suddenly she is your daughter?" Carolyn was not backing down.

"Don't think I'm going to sit back this time and watch her fuck you!"

"Matt! You are disgusting," Carolyn said as she turned to leave.

"You make me sick!"

Carolyn turned around to face him. "The feeling is mutual." She turned around and walked out.

Later on that evening he told her he would be away for two days. Carolyn breathed in a sigh of relief. She actually felt a weight lift off her shoulder as she heard him close the door behind him as he left.

* * * * * * * * * * * * * * * * * *

Carolyn answered the phone as she rushed into the house with a few packages, putting them down on the counter in front of her.

"Hello?"

"Hi."

Silence followed.

"I would like....I need to see you," Raisa said abruptly.

"Why don't you come for lunch," Carolyn invited her tensely.

"All right," Raisa sounded disappointed.

"Do you know where I live?"

"Yes."

"Come then."

"Now?"

"Yes."

Carolyn heard the dial tone and hung up.

****

It seemed like time had stopped and suddenly Raisa stood in front of her. They were both in a daze lost in each other's eyes.

"Do you like tomato soup?"

"Never tried it"

Raisa walked closer and closer and Carolyn kept talking. "Well, it's nice and warm. I'm also making you a nice sandw--" Suddenly she was engulfed by Raisa's mouth.

And the fire that had lay dormant for so long became a raging inferno that could no longer be contained by the conventions and prejudices of life. Carolyn's hands went up to the dark mane of hair, and, as she did, her head fell back and Raisa kissed her down her neck.

Raisa's hands sought the skin that once had given her so much pleasure, her hand sliding under Carolyn's blouse, finding its target in Carolyn's breast. She moaned with such pleasure that it touched her very soul. Carolyn groaned as well and mouths met once again.

"Mom, I'm home."

Raisa and Carolyn pulled apart immediately. Simon walked in and saw the tenseness in their faces as they stood a bare foot or two apart from one another.

"I'm sorry," he said not exactly knowing why he said it.

151

Carolyn turned around and tried to straighten her hair and blouse.

Raisa turned and walked towards Simon and put her hand out trying to give Carolyn a moment to pull herself together.

"Hello, Simon."

"Hi," he said, a smile appearing on his face as he looked from her to his mother.

"Your mother invited me to lunch," she said, a little embarrassed and finding it hard to look at him straight in the eyes.

Carolyn turned around and looked in astonishment. "Simon, this is Raisa."

"Hi," Simon said theatrically. "I know who she is, mom," he added with a smile. "Amanda likes you," he said to Raisa.

"I like her, too," Raisa replied with a smile on her face that seemed to shine with happiness.

Carolyn looked at them in surprise as she saw the bantering back and forth.

"Do I smell tomato soup?"

"That's what your mother said." Raisa smiled even more now and looked at Carolyn. Carolyn stared back and shook her head as she laughed out loud.

"Follow me to the kitchen you two." She walked past them, and Simon and Raisa followed behind laughing.

Chapter Twenty-Five

"Well, that was great. Thank you for lunch," Raisa said, suddenly getting up. Carolyn stood beside her.

"Did you come in a cab?"

"Actually, I did," she said with a smile looking deeply into Carolyn's eyes..

"Simon can take you back," Carolyn said, both women seemed unable to break eye contact.

Simon smiled looking from one to the other and decided to interfere.

"Mom, I can pick up Amanda and we can order something in if you want to spend some more time catching up."

Raisa looked at Simon with a big smile on her face and he smiled back. Carolyn could not believe what she was seeing.

"Why do I have the feeling I am being bushwhacked?"

"Us?" Simon and Raisa said in unison and all three started laughing.

"Okay, I'll give you a lift back to your hotel," Carolyn finally said. "Simon, no McDonald's, okay?"

"Oh Mom."

Raisa touched her arm and Carolyn saw the begging smile in her face as well. "Okay, Simon. But just this once."

"Yes! I owe you," he said to Raisa.

"You have lots of credit," she said with a smile.

****

Carolyn went up to the penthouse with Raisa. She had not been asked, it was just understood. The silent language between them was coming back faster than they could decipher it.

"When will you return to Venezuela?" Carolyn asked as she looked down. She had sat down at the other end of the couch.

"No hurry. No one waiting for me," Raisa stated simply.

"Of course they are. You have Andrea's son and Nona," Carolyn said indignantly.

"Antonio is in boarding school in Switzerland and Nona…she died four weeks ago," Raisa said as she got up and walked to the glass wall.

Carolyn allowed the impact of the words to sink in. *Nona is dead.*

Suddenly, Raisa felt two arms come from behind her. For a moment she hesitated and then she allowed love to come in. She melted into those arms that held her up from behind and she leaned into their strength.

Carolyn could almost feel when Raisa's legs gave out. They both sat on the floor as she hung on tightly to the woman in her arms. Raisa began to cry in earnest and Carolyn held her tightly.

The dark head fell back as the saddest sobs Carolyn had ever heard a human being make were heard. Finally, she had been allowed in. Raisa was trusting her with her pain and her heart. The woman she loved became both child and adult and all the pain she had held inside her for so long came out with every tear and every sob that racked her body.

The room that had been covered in sunlight was now covered in darkness. Carolyn held Raisa closely to her tightly still. Raisa had fallen asleep in her arms sometime ago.

Carolyn now realized that she had seen the signs. Raisa seemed sadder, softer and yes, more vulnerable to those that had eyes and cared enough to look. She was hurting inside. And this time she had no safety net to run to. Carolyn held her tighter and Raisa stirred.

Raisa tried sitting up. She looked around disoriented and once her eyes met Carolyn's they filled with tears again and she went into her embrace. "Don't go, please Cara, don't go."

"I won't leave," Carolyn reassured her. "Come, let me take care of you."

Carolyn got up and held her hand out. Raisa looked up and gave her hand without hesitation.

****

Carolyn ran the shower and helped Raisa undress. She helped her into the shower and as she was about to close the door Raisa reached for her. "You won't go?"

"No, I'll be right back," Carolyn said reassuringly.

Carolyn called Simon and explained that she would probably be very late. He assured her that all was fine and to be as late as she needed to be.

Carolyn hung up the phone and smiled. Simon was full of surprises. Somehow she knew he had had something to do with the turn of events in her life.

****

Raisa did not hear the shower door open. She only felt those same arms that had held her before come up from behind her and hold her now. She leaned back into them.

Carolyn washed her body lovingly and washed her hair. She dried her and walked her to bed. Raisa allowed her to take care of her, as she had always wanted to. But instead of giving Carolyn joy it only brought her sadness to see the broken heart that lay in front of her.

Carolyn removed Raisa's robe and helped her into bed. Raisa

held a hand out to her pleadingly. Carolyn removed her own robe and got into bed with her. She realized that this connection that Raisa was begging for was much more than sexual; she needed it to survive.

Carolyn took her into her arms and caressed her until she heard the sounds of her sleep. She continued to caress her even as she slept.

In the middle of the night, Raisa sat up and screamed in fear.

Carolyn was there behind her reassuring her and pulling her back into the world.

Raisa turned in that embrace and looked into the face that had haunted her dreams for so many lonely years and her hand reached out to touch it.

Carolyn kissed her fingers before Raisa pulled them away. Carolyn's mouth then leaned forward and found the lips she sought. The kiss was soft and welcoming.

Carolyn pulled her closer and Raisa melted into her embrace. They made love slowly and in no rush. Their lovemaking was slow and tender, full of caresses and of giving more than taking mixed with tears and smiles. Kisses with promises of surrender and of glorious union. Both women gave and took of one another. And somewhere during the night they found something that had been lost.

Chapter Twenty-Six

Carolyn walked into her garden in the early hours of the morning.   She had left Raisa in bed, still asleep.   She ran her fingers through her hair as a feeling of an old tiredness took hold of her heart. She could no longer deny her need for Raisa. She had run once before, she would not run again.   But somehow, it all seemed so much more urgent now.   The only way to show someone you love them is to yell it to the four winds and not care who hears it.

Carolyn turned around and went inside. She sat down on the sofa patiently until the morning had finally arrived in all its glory.

Simon found her early in the morning sitting quietly.   He walked up to her cautiously. "Mom? You okay?"

"Come, sit with me," she patted the sofa next to her. "I do love her."

"I know."

"Amanda?"

"She will be fine with it," Simon reassured her.   "I think Raisa and Amanda will be good for one another, too."

Carolyn looked at Simon once again in wonder.   "I must have done something really good to get you," she said to her son as her hand caressed his face.

"You did Mom, you loved me. It's was my turn to show you I love you too."

Carolyn let the tears run down her cheeks as she held her son

157

to her.

"I knew you had some hand in this," she laughed between the tears.

"Not me mom, she came back on her own," Simon assured her.

****

Carolyn walked into the Copeco building with a firm stride and a determination that showed in every step. She walked past all the secretaries and straight through the 11th floor.

She saw the surprised look of the last secretary as she tried to pass by her and succeeded in between her to the door of the boardroom. She had called earlier and she had been informed that Raisa was in a meeting.

Carolyn walked straight in; all in the room turned to face her. Oddly enough, Matt was seated at the table as well. Perhaps it would have been prudent to wait, but she had waited ten years and that was long enough.

Raisa stood up and waited. Carolyn took a deep breath.

"You made me an offer ten years ago, or at least you were going to. Is it still on the table?"

"Carolyn!" Matt stood up quickly

"Yes," Raisa answered simply. Both women could only see the other.

"Carolyn, this is not the time or the place." Matt was visibly agitated, looking around at all the people seated around the boardroom intently staring.

Carolyn and Raisa stood as if they were the only two people in the room.

"I shouldn't have run away," Carolyn said softly

"I should have gone after you," Raisa answered quickly.

Not a word or a sound was heard from anyone seated around the table. They were all looking around at each other and in Matt's direction in embarrassment.

"I'm still afraid," Carolyn said.

"I know."

"Do you still want me?"

"Oh God, Carolyn, I never stopped." And Carolyn could see the truth of that statement in Raisa's eyes.

"I don't have to...." Matt slammed his papers down and began to leave.

"Sit down!" Matt hesitated for a moment then obeyed. "Everyone get out! Now!"

All the board members hurried to get out. When they all had, Raisa turned her full attention to Matt.

Raisa opened her brief case and pushed a folder towards him.

"Look it over; I believe I am being generous." Raisa looked at him with a murderous glare. "I would rather just kill you but Carolyn would probably object to that type of behavior and, for better or worse, you are Simon's and Amanda's father. But don't push too hard, Matt. Never push me too hard!"

Raisa looked up and met Carolyn's gaze again. At that moment Carolyn was not sure whether Raisa was being sarcastic or just plain honest. Matt looked like he believed her threat. Raisa then looked towards Matt again.

"Sign these papers and all in that package is yours." She placed some document in front of him that she took out of her briefcase.

"What am I signing?"

"Does it matter?"

Matt looked at the folder and was visibly pleased and smiled at Raisa. He then looked over the papers he was to sign.

"I won't..." he started to say.

"It's all or nothing," Raisa spat. "There will be no negotiations."

"I won't give up my son or my daughter," he said indignantly. "Simon is older and I know that he will want to go with her, but I'll fight for Amanda's custody in the courts and I'll get it, too."

"Another five million," Raisa said without batting an eye. Carolyn began to feel unwell as she stared from one to the other.

"Seven."

"Done, now sign!" Raisa demanded as she pointed to the

papers in front of them on the table.

Matt signed the papers and walked towards Carolyn.

"Not a word!" Raisa warned him. "One word will cost you my patience and your life."

Matt turned to stare at her in disdain.

"She chose me," Raisa savored those words. "You say one word to her, just one, and no matter how much she pleads, nothing will save you. Because Matt, this time I **will** kill you."

Matt stood silently, then turned around and walked out.

"The papers?" Carolyn asked softly.

"They were drawn up to set you free."

"You were very sure of yourself," Carolyn stated

"Not sure, just hopeful," Raisa said earnestly "I have been living on hopes my whole life. This time I fought for my happiness."

Raisa looked at Carolyn intensely now. Carolyn saw as the clouds disappeared in those beautiful blue eyes and all that she could see was love. And she remembered the words that Nona had once said to her and she smiled.

"I'm trying, Cara mia," Raisa tried to say reassuringly.

"I see," Carolyn said with a smile.

They both started walking slowly towards one another. Raisa now stood a few feet in front of her.

"I would ask again." Raisa took a deep breath, another step and then only their breathing stood between them. Carolyn smiled and waited for the question.

"Would you be mine forever and ever?"

"Yes."

And the distance closed visibly before them as two lovers' lips united together forever at last.

THE END.

About the Author

S. Anne Gardner is the pseudonym of a woman who has created her own world to her liking. Though she has lived all over the world and had more experiences than she probably wanted, she has survived with the constant desire to protect those she loves. That would include her wife and life partner, Lisa, their three sons, three cats and a handful of amazing friends. Anne lives on the East Coast, makes her living in insurance, and spends her spare time reading and writing, among other things. Her love of communication and discussion makes it easy for those who have read her stories to talk with her. She loves to hear from everyone, so please feel free to email her at sanneo17@aol.com and visit her web page at www.geminifiction.com .

Compensation

by S. Anne Gardner

Victoria's fist hit the desktop. She was furious. This deal had cost her two million dollars. Someone had dropped the ball. She was a vicious businesswoman. No one ever got the better of her. This had caught her off guard. Someone close to her had failed and now she would have to personally pick up the pieces and crucify the culprit. Her temper was legendary. All four men who stood in front her, stood in fear.

"What the hell happened here Grant?" She asked with barely restraint anger. "You were in charge of this. What happened? When I handed this over to you the deal was sealed. What the fuck happened?"

All three men started speaking at once. She sat down and just stared in controlled anger. They were her puppets. The plan was in action. It had worked faster than she had anticipated. It tasted sweet; so sweet that she had to restrain herself from licking her lips in pleasure.

She had dreamed about how this moment would feel. She had planned it meticulously. It would happen this way, this would result from it. She had even planned sitting as she was and watching it unfold. She could taste the anger and the pleasure in her mouth. She continued to stare at these caricatures in front of her in disdain.

Suddenly, she had heard enough. Victoria rose to her feet and all three men held their breath in silence.

"Get out!" Victoria growled. Grant was about to open his mouth and just as quickly shut it. Sometimes fighting another day was better than loosing one's job. All three men filed out of the office without muttering another word.

She walked around her desk and stopped in front of a portrait to the side wall. The resemblance to the woman on the portrait was unquestionable. Jessika Morlen had been breathtakingly beautiful. "Now I am just like you mother. The game has truly begun," she said softly. "I will make you proud. I will out do even you."

~~~~~~~~~~

"Come on Danni, give me your hand. I promise I won't let go," the dark haired child coaxed.

"Tory, I'm afraid," Danni answered fearfully as she hung by a branch about 10 feet off the ground.

Tory was two branches higher leaning over with an extended hand.

"I promise. I won't let go, no matter what."

"Promise?" Danni asked

"Promise," Tory assured her.

"No, I can't do it Tory, I'm too scared." Danni hugged the branch she was now lying on. Quiet suddenly, the cracking became audible. The blonde haired child looked up into fear filled violet eyes.

"Danni! The branch is breaking give me your hand!!" Tory yelled. The cracking noises became louder and a scream filled the air.

Danni had reached out before the branch had finally fallen and now swung in mid air being held up by the grip of her friend. Blue eyes filled with fear held onto violet determined ones.

"Hold on! I won't let go. Try to grab the branch nearby as I try to swing you over," said Tory between her teeth.

"Tory, don't let go please, don't let go," Danni begged.

"Never, I promised."

Danni was able to reach the branch and both girls gradually worked their way down the tree. As they reached the ground they sat down leaning on the tree trunk, both still filled with the excitement and the fear of what just had happened. Tory looked over to Danni.

2

"Are you okay?" Tory asked.

"Yeah, I thought I was going to die. You saved my life, you know" Danni's eyes filled with admiration.

Tory just gave her a slumped over smile. Danni suddenly noticed that Tory's shirt had blood on it. She looked down at Tory's hands and saw the cuts in them

"Oh my God Tory! Your hands! They're all cut up!" Danni's shocked eyes looked into a face that had revealed nothing.

"I cut them on the branch," Tory stated simply.

"When you were hanging on to me wasn't it?"

"I promised. I promised I wouldn't let you go, and I didn't" Tory stated proudly.

"Does it hurt?"

"Yeah, a little" Tory said as she lifted her shoulders. Danni took both hands into her own and brought them up to her lips and kissed them lightly. Tory just stared in adoration.

"Thank you for not letting me fall." Danni kissed the dark haired child on the cheek. Tory smiled and looked down at her hands. "Will you get punished?"

"It doesn't matter," Tory answered softly. "I'll tell them it was my fault."

"No, it'll make it worse for you."

"I'm in trouble anyway. I don't want you to get in trouble," Tory said quickly." Mother will be mad and I'll get punished but I won't get hit like you for climbing that tree."

Danni looked down as tears started falling down her cheeks. "Danni, I promise I'll tell them it was all my fault," Tory insisted. Danni looked up with tear-filled eyes. "One day when I am big I won't let your father ever hurt you again. I promise," Tory said as she reached out and embraced the smaller child. "One day, we will leave together."

~~~~~~~~~~

Victoria closed her eyes and pushed the memory back where it belonged. Why had she suddenly remembered that? It was such a long time ago. Another lifetime really. A memory that had betrayed her. She shook her head, wanting to dislodge it from her mind. It was about someone that she could have been but that could now never be. She closed her eyes and when she opened them, again they were filled with the vision of the portrait.

3

"I hate you Mother. God, how I hate you."

~~~~~~~~

"Father what happened?"

"We're ruined," Tom answered.

"Ruined how?" Danielle insisted.

"We are going to file chapter 11 Danielle, what part of that don't you understand?" Tom yelled.

"What happened? Just a few days ago you went out of your way during dinner to tell us how well the company was doing."

"I'm in real trouble." Tom sat down and ran his fingers through his hair.

"Father…what happened?"

"Victoria Morlen, that's what happened!" Danielle straightened up as her father spoke. What did any of this have to do with Victoria Morlen? She hadn't heard that name in years.

"What does Victoria have to do with this?"

"She's taking over all of my notes with the bank" Tom growled as he got up and started pacing the room. "That bitch is destroying me. She won't even accept my phone calls."

Danielle sat down and the silence filled the room. The only thing that kept going around in her head was that Victoria was back. The last time that they had seen each other had been horrible. There had been so much anger. Victoria said that she hated her and she would be back. Well, she was back. Danielle had so many questions. Victoria had been her friend when they were children. Then, it all changed. Victoria changed. The last thing she remembered was Victoria's eyes and the hatred in them.

~~~~~~~~

"Sit down Dominic," Victoria commanded.

"Here is all the information you requested. What do you want me to do?" Dominic asked after putting a folder on the desk in front of her.

"Show me."

He took the file and started to explain. He first placed a photo of Thomas Deveraux Jenkins in front of her.

"He is hooked, line and sinker, as they say. Not only do we have him for embezzlement but for getting creative with his books. I just finished buying all his bank notes a few days ago," Dominic said with a smile. Victoria nodded and he placed the next photo in front of her.

"Beatrice J. Jenkins has not been very involved in anything except for some charity functions she attends. She has been having some heart problems for the last 5 years or so. What should I do with her?" Dominic asked as Victoria finished going through some of the photos attached to Tom's photograph. She threw one at Dominic.

"Send her that one. Keep the prettier ones for later," Victoria said with a smile. Dominic looked at the photo of Tom Jenkins kissing a very attractive blonde and nodded.

He placed the next photo and history in front of her.

"This is Tom Jr. Pretty boy about town. A real hell raiser. He is in his sophomore year of college. He has gotten in some trouble but nothing very serious. The old man always comes in and bails him out. What about him?"

"Scandal and jail time, Dominic. This is Tom's pride and joy. Make it rape and jail. I want this to hurt," Victoria finished saying with a scowl on her face.

"Done." Dominic then put the next photo in front of her.

There in front of her were the eyes from long ago. The face had changed, of course. Danielle was now a woman. All she could remember were the features of a child. However, the eyes -- they had not changed. The face that stared back at her was simply beautiful. Victoria stared at the photograph and heard nothing of what Dominic was saying. Danielle, her Danielle, was now a beautiful woman.

"What do you want me to do with her?" Dominic asked.

"What?"

"Her? What do I do with her?" Dominic repeated. He looked at Victoria, puzzled. It was not like her to phase out like that.

"Tell me about her again," Victoria asked calmly,

"Danielle Jenkins is a painter. She has an exhibition scheduled at a local gallery in two months. She is engaged to Paul Hendrick..."

"She's what?"

Dominic looked up in surprise. He had hit a nerve.

"She's engaged to Paul Hendrick," Dominic repeated and stared as Victoria got up walked up to the window and stared out in silence. He waited. He knew better than to interrupt when she exploded like this.

She stood there for what seemed like a lifetime, deep in her memories; as usual unreadable. But Dominic had seen something others never got a chance to. He saw Victoria Morlen shaken. He waited patiently and said nothing as she walked back to her desk and sat down again.

"What do I do with her?" Dominic asked.

"Nothing," she said looking out into space.

"Nothing?"

"What part of nothing don't you understand?" Victoria growled as she now stared at him.

"Ahhh...." Dominic mumbled.

Victoria got up very quickly. And all the anger that she was famous for could be now seen in those violet eyes.

"Listen to me carefully Dominic. Don't think I don't know that you are always picking at my table. This one is different. Do you understand?" Victoria yelled.

"Okay, fine. This one strikes your fancy. I can understand that," Dominic said all too quickly. Victoria came around the desk quicker than he had ever seen her and was now face to face with him. Dominic was afraid of his cousin for the first time in his life.

"Stay away from her! She is mine!" Victoria said through her teeth barely able to control the anger from spilling over. "Say it! Say it!"

"Yes Victoria, she is yours."

She quickly stepped away from him. She turned her back to Dominic before she spoke again, this time in control again. "Go, and do what I asked. Dominic, dig up all you can on this Paul Hendricks." She turned when she heard the door close.

Victoria looked at the closed door and then back at the photograph. She walked slowly back to her desk and sat down as her fingertips traveled over the face on the photo. She was surprised to hear the word that escaped her lips.

"Danni......" The name was barely a whisper.

~~~~~~~~~

"Dad?"

Tommy? What's wrong?" Tom asked.

6

"I'm in jail Dad. Jesus, Dad, you have to help me. I'm in real trouble. I didn't do anything. I swear it. I'm being charged with rape, Dad. Jesus! I didn't do it. I swear I didn't do it!"

"Calm down Tommy. Where are you?" Tom quickly wrote all the information down. "I'm calling Alistair and we will get you out of there. Stay calm son. I'm on my way. And Tommy, don't say anything. Do you hear? Don't say a thing until I get there with Alistair."

"Okay, Dad. Okay."

~~~~~~~~~~

Beatrice heard Tom run out of the house and watched as he got into his car and drive away. She proceeded to the library to go through the mail as she did at this time everyday. Her eye was caught by a large envelope with no return address. She turned it over opened it. Out of the envelope slid a photograph. Beatrice recognized Tom immediately. Her breathing became ragged and she clutched at her chest. She managed to get to the house phone and touched the alarm button before she collapse to the floor.

The emergency buttons had been installed in case of such a situation. Beatrice had a very weak heart. Immediately the staff responded. Danielle heard it and started running down the stairs. She saw the maid run into the library and she followed. They both found the older woman lying unconscious on the floor.

"Esther, hurry call 911!" Urged Danielle as she ran to her mother. "Mom, Oh God, Mom. Can you hear me?" Danielle asked as she put her mother's head on her lap. Danielle noticed that crumpled in one of her mother's hands was a photograph. She took it and as she saw what must have upset her mother. The photograph was of a very attractive blonde and her father engaged in a very passionate kiss. Danielle looked down at her mother and shook her head. "Oh Mom, please be all right." She stroked her mother's hair in understanding. Within seconds the sirens filled the air.

~~~~~~~~~~

Tom and his daughter stood in opposite ends of the Intensive Coronary Care Unit's waiting room. Both deep in their own thoughts.

Danielle had never been particularly close to her father. She had too many unresolved issues with him. But, she loved her mother

7

dearly. She had always run interference between them. And now that she knew why her mother had had this attack she was angry.

"Where's Tommy?"

"He is not able to be here just yet," Tom answered without looking at his daughter.

"What do you mean he can't be here just yet? Did you call him Dad?" Danielle demanded.

"He's in jail. Alistair is getting bail."

"What? What is going on with this family? Why is he in jail?"

"False charges."

"What charges Dad?"

"Rape, they are accusing him of rape," Tom finally said now looking at his daughter's shocked face. "He didn't do it. He said he didn't."

"God, this will kill mother," Danielle said softly as she ran her fingers though her hair in a defeated gesture. She sat down and covered her face with both hands. Tom looked on and said nothing as he turned around and looked out the window and into the night.

~~~~~~~~~

Above the same sky across town was a woman battling her own demons. Victoria was looking out into the city before her. She was in the penthouse suite of the Ritz Carlton Hotel. She had called Caroline earlier and placed her order. She was a good customer and Caroline only ever sent the best. So when there was a knock on the door Victoria called out without hesitation knowing exactly what to expect.

"Come in," Victoria called out without turning around. The door opened and closed behind her. "I fee very restless tonight. I will need you all night."

"I'm here for as long as you want me," replied a soft sensual voice. Victoria turned around and visually assessed the woman in front of her.

"Your hair is dark."

"Did you want a blonde or ..."

"No, I don't want a blonde. You will do," Victoria said as she walked over to the brunette. "Take off your clothes."

~~~~~~~~~

"It could have been worse, Tom. She is responding to treatment. It's hard to tell what the damage is right now. She's holding her own.

8

I'll come out again in a few hours to talk to you and Danielle," Doctor Mc Murphy said turning toward Danielle. "You did the right thing when you got her to take the aspirin. It helped with the coagulation."

"John, what do you think?"

"I think your mother is a strong woman."

"Thank you, John."

"I'll be out later to talk to you okay?" Dr Mc Murphy said as he walked back into the ICCU. Danielle walked back to the opposite side of the room from her father.

"She got a photograph today," Danielle said not looking in her father's direction.

"What photograph?"

"Of you and a woman in a passionate kiss," Danielle said accusingly, still not looking at her father. "She had it in her hand when she collapsed. I saw it too." She looked up.

Tom said nothing then quite suddenly he looked angry. "Who could have sent it? Damn, everything is coming out wrong lately."

"Coming out wrong? My mother is in there because of you!"

"How dare you talk to me like that!" He growled.

"I stopped caring what you did a long time ago Dad, but she does. She still believes you," Danielle said, not backing down.

"I have no idea who might have sent that."

"No, of course not. You never know anything. Things just happen."

Both faced away from one another in their respective corners.

~~~~~~~~~~

"What do you have on Paul Hendriks?"

"Our boy Paul is a clean cut boy. Very boring, like his fiancée. His papa however has plenty." Dominic handed the file over to Victoria.

"Well, well. His papa is no other than Senator Matthew Hendricks from the state of Iowa. Papa has been busy hasn't he?" Victoria's face lit up with a bright smile.

"He has indeed," Dominic smiled in return.

~~~~~~~~~~

The telephone rang and Tom picked up quickly. He was waiting for a call from Alistair. He was not able to raise the money to bail Tommy out and he was trying to figure out how he would get out of

9

all this. His world was falling apart in front of him everywhere he looked.

"Tom," purred a voice.

"Who is this?"

"This is Victoria Morlen. I think we should talk."

"Victoria, yes. When?" Tom said quickly.

"Now."

"Now?"

"Unless you have something better to do," Victoria said nonchalantly.

"No. Now is fine."

"I'll be there in 30 seconds."

"30 seconds?"

"Yes, that is how long it will take me."

Tom was thrown of balance. This was a game he had played often. But he was on the wrong end this time. Before he was able to say anything the front door bell rang.

"Open the door Tom." The telephone line went dead. Tom looked down at the phone and up again as the doorbell rang once more.

He opened the door to his study as the maid opened the front door. He was taken aback when he saw a ghost from his past walk into his house. He stood motionless as Victoria approached him. He took in a deep breath. Before him stood the very image of Jessika Morlen.

"Hello Tom," purred Victoria holding out her hand. Tom looked down at it and took it. He said nothing as she quickly released it and walked into his study leaving him standing there staring at her in shock as she walked further into the room. She turned around and stared at him.

"I hear you have been looking for me?" Victoria said as she sat down on a nearby chair.

"Ahh...Yes. It would seem that you control the most shares to my company."

"I control what used to be your company."

"Technically..."

"No technically Tom. It is now my company. Sit down!"

He walked over to a chair in front of her and sat down. "What do you want?"

"You can't give me what I want." Victoria's smile faded.

"Perhaps we can work out a deal," he attempted again.

"What deal? How will you return my two million, Tom?" Victoria asked. Tom's face went white with shock. "How will you get your son out of jail with no money? And I did hear about poor Beatrice. It would seem that your life is slowly falling apart." Victoria smiled.

Tom stared in disbelief. "You! Why are you doing this? You are the one responsible for all this aren't you?" Victoria leaned back and smiled again.

"Did you send my mother that photograph?" Victoria looked toward the voice coming from the opened study door. In walked Danielle. "Did you send that photo to my mother?" she asked once more. Victoria recovered quickly.

"Yes."

Danielle stared at her in horror. Before her was once upon a time the only person she had ever confided in. They had shared secrets and dreams. This could not be Tory. This was not her friend. This woman that stood before her was cold. Danielle went up to her and slapped her across the face hard. Victoria's face turned back and stared at Danielle in controlled anger. When Danielle's hand went to strike her again it was stopped in midair. Both women stood looking at each other until Danielle pulled away.

"What happened to you? When did you turn into such an animal?" Danielle said in disgust.

Victoria smiled. "When I lost my family." Danielle stared not understanding. "You have grown up nicely, Danielle," Victoria said as she looked Danielle up and down.

Danielle was taken aback.

"Yes, very nice" Victoria purred. Victoria walked up to Danielle and her hand went up to her shoulder and traveled down over Danielle's breast and rib cage. Danielle inhaled audibly and took a step away quickly backing straight into her father.

"She's not a fruit off the old tree, is she Tom?" Victoria said as she turned around and put some distance between them before she turned to face them again. Her eyes went in search of Danielle's. Victoria smiled.

11

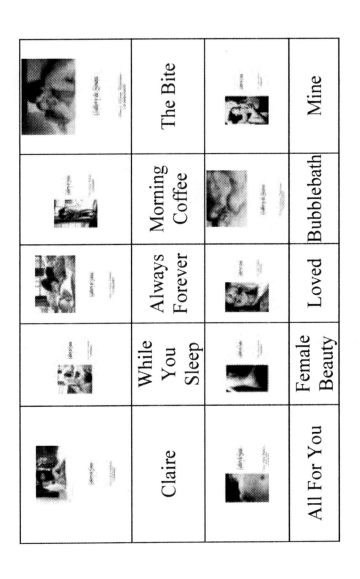

	While You Sleep	Always Forever	Morning Coffee	The Bite
Claire				
	Female Beauty	Loved	Bubblebath	Mine
All For You				

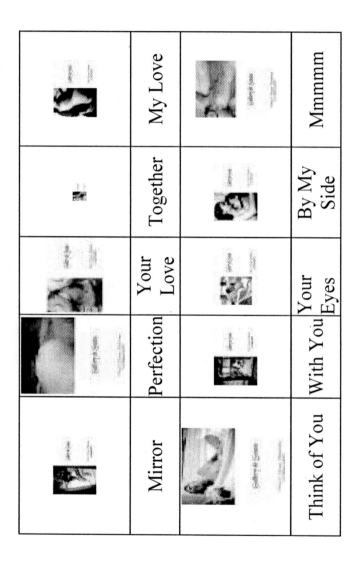

Think of You	Mirror	Perfection	Your Love	Together	My Love
	With You	Your Eyes		By My Side	Mmmmm

Unless otherwise specified the cards will come blank, with no printing inside. You may, however, request something be printed inside at no extra cost.

Personalizing the cards will be done upon request or you may choose to have a pre-determined text printed.

- Photo Cards are $5.00 each US funds or $4.00 each when purchased in lots of 10 or more. Shipping is $.75 per card within the continental US Shipping outside the United States will be determined on an individual basis so that we may charge you only the actual shipping cost. At Dare 2 Dream you will never be charged a handling fee.

- Post Cards are $3.50 each US funds or $3.00 each when purchased in lots of 10 or more. Shipping is $.50 per card within the continental US For shipping outside the United States, see photo cards.

- 8 X 10 Photos of the images are available in glossy or matte finish for $8.00 each US funds Shipping is $1.50 per print within the continental United States For shipping outside the United States, see photo cards.

South Carolina residents add 5% sales tax.

Learn more about the photographer and the Gallery de Souza

Visit our website at: http://limitlessd2d.net/index.html

Please mail your orders with a check or money order to:

Limitless Corporation, Dare 2 Dream Publications
100 Pin Oak Ct.
Lexington, SC 29073-7911

Please make checks or money orders payable to: Limitless.

Tom interrupted Victoria's game. "What do you want Victoria?" She looked to him now. Victoria's eyebrow went up in question.

"Are you asking me?"

"What do you want?" Tom growled. Victoria became very serious. Tom stood holding his breath suddenly realizing he was in a game he would not win. Danielle could see the tension in her father.

Victoria smiled again. Her eyes went to Danielle's. "Think about it" and as she said this she walked out and left father and daughter stunned. Danielle turned and saw the front door close as Victoria walked out.

~~~~~~~~~

Compensation will be released later this year by Limitless Corporation, Dare 2 Dream Publishing. Be sure to watch our website for dates.

www.limitlessd2d.net

Introducing...
Art By Joy

By JoyArgento

Hi, allow me to introduce myself. My name is Joy Argento and I am the artist on all of these pieces. I have been doing artwork since I was a small child. That gives me about 35 years of experience. I majored in art in high school and took a few college art courses. Most of my work is done in either pencil or airbrush mixed with color pencils. I have recently added designing and creating artwork on the computer. Some of the work featured on these pages were created and "painted" on the computer. I am self taught in this as well as in the use of the airbrush.

I have been selling my art for the last 15 years and have had my work featured on trading cards, prints and in magazines. I have sold in galleries and to private collectors from all around the world.

I live in Western New York with my three kids, four cats, one dog and the love of my life. It is definitely a full house. I appreciate you taking the time to check out my artwork. Please feel free to email me with your thoughts or questions. Custom orders are always welcomed too.

Contact me at ArtByJoy@aol.com . I look forward to hearing from you.

Making Love

Towel Cuddling

Motorcycle Women

Joy Argento

Check out her work at
LimitlessD2D or at her website.
Remember: ArtByJoy@aol.com !

Order These Great Books Directly From Limitless, Dare 2 Dream Publishing

The Amazon Queen by L M Townsend	20.00	
Define Destiny by J M Dragon	20.00	The one that started it all…
Desert Hawk, revised by Katherine E. Standelll	18.00	Many new scenes
Golden Gate by Erin Jennifer Mar	18.00	
The Brass Ring **By Mavis Applewater**	18.00	HOT
Haunting Shadows by J M Dragon	18.00	
Spirit Harvest by Trish Shields	15.00	
PWP: Plot? What Plot? by Mavis Applewater	18.00	HOT
Journeys **By Anne Azel**	18.00	NEW
Memories Kill By S. B. Zarben	20.00	
Up The River, revised **By Sam Ruskin**	18.00	Many new scenes
	Total	

South Carolina residents add 5% sales tax.
Domestic shipping is $3.50 per book

Visit our website at: http://limitlessd2d.net

Please mail your orders with credit card info, check or money order to:

Limitless, Dare 2 Dream Publishing
100 Pin Oak Ct.
Lexington, SC 29073-7911

Please make checks or money orders payable to: Limitless.

I

Order More Great Books Directly From Limitless, Dare 2 Dream Publishing

Title	Price	Note
Daughters of Artemis by L M Townsend	18.00	
Connecting Hearts By Val Brown and MJ Walker	18.00	
Mysti: Mistress of Dreams **By Sam Ruskin**	18.00	HOT
Family Connections **By Val Brown & MJ Walker**	18.00	Sequel to Connecting Hearts
A Thousand Shades of Feeling by Carolyn McBride	18.00	
The Amazon Nation **By Carla Osborne**	18.00	Great for research
Poetry from the Featherbed **By pinfeather**	18.00	If you think you hate poetry you haven't read this
None So Blind, 3rd Edition By LJ Maas	16.00	NEW
A Saving Solace **By DS Bauden**	18.00	NEW
Return of the Warrior By Katherine E. Standell	20.00	Sequel to Desert Hawk
Journey's End **By LJ Maas**	18.00	NEW
	Total	

South Carolina residents add 5% sales tax.
Domestic shipping is $3.50 per book
Please mail your orders with credit card info, check or money order to:
Limitless, Dare 2 Dream Publishing
100 Pin Oak Ct.
Lexington, SC 29073-7911
Please make checks or money orders payable to: Limitless.

Name:
Address:
Address:
City/State/Zip:
Country:
Phone:
Credit Card Type:
CC Number:
EXP Date:
List Items Ordered and Retail Prices:

List Items Ordered and Retail Prices:

You may also send a money order or check. Please make
payments out to: Limitless Corporation.
You may Fax this form to us at: 803-359-2881 or mail it
to:
Limitless Corporation
100 Pin Oak Court
Lexington, SC 29073-7911

South Carolina residents add 5% sales tax.
Domestic shipping is $3.50 per book

Visit our website at: http://limitlessd2d.net

II

Printed in the United States
21076LVS00005B/79-102

9 780974 412160